D0485464

"You mean…i
to be like tha

Damiano splayed long fingers around her cheekbones, gazing deep into her incredulous green eyes. "You just would not relax. You had so many hang-ups. You hit my male ego right where it hurts. The only woman I couldn't satisfy was my wife."

Eden stifled a groan. *The only woman I couldn't satisfy was my wife.* One very revealing statement from a male of Damiano's sophistication and experience, she reflected in strong dismay.

"It didn't matter to me enough…I didn't understand," she muttered in a tone of feverish regret, kissing his shoulder in belated apology. She had almost lost him. But he had chosen to come back to her and give their marriage another chance….

LYNNE GRAHAM was born in Northern Ireland and has been a keen romance reader since her teens. She is very happily married to an understanding husband, who has learned to cook since she started to write! Her five children keep her on her toes. She has a very large old English sheepdog, which knocks everything over, and two cats. When time allows, Lynne is a keen gardener.

Books by Lynne Graham

Don't miss any of our special offers. Write to us at the following address for information on our newest releases.

Harlequin Reader Service
U.S.: 3010 Walden Ave., P.O. Box 1325, Buffalo, NY 14269
Canadian: P.O. Box 609, Fort Erie, Ont. L2A 5X3

CS

Lynne Graham

DAMIANO'S RETURN

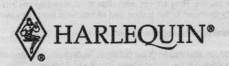

HARLEQUIN®

TORONTO • NEW YORK • LONDON
AMSTERDAM • PARIS • SYDNEY • HAMBURG
STOCKHOLM • ATHENS • TOKYO • MILAN • MADRID
PRAGUE • WARSAW • BUDAPEST • AUCKLAND

If you purchased this book without a cover you should be aware
that this book is stolen property. It was reported as "unsold and
destroyed" to the publisher, and neither the author nor the
publisher has received any payment for this "stripped book."

ISBN 0-373-12163-6

DAMIANO'S RETURN

First North American Publication 2001.

Copyright © 2000 by Lynne Graham.

All rights reserved. Except for use in any review, the reproduction or
utilization of this work in whole or in part in any form by any electronic,
mechanical or other means, now known or hereafter invented, including
xerography, photocopying and recording, or in any information storage
or retrieval system, is forbidden without the written permission of the
publisher, Harlequin Enterprises Limited, 225 Duncan Mill Road,
Don Mills, Ontario, Canada M3B 3K9.

All characters in this book have no existence outside the imagination of
the author and have no relation whatsoever to anyone bearing the same
name or names. They are not even distantly inspired by any individual
known or unknown to the author, and all incidents are pure invention.

This edition published by arrangement with Harlequin Books S.A.

® and TM are trademarks of the publisher. Trademarks indicated with
® are registered in the United States Patent and Trademark Office, the
Canadian Trade Marks Office and in other countries.

Visit us at www.eHarlequin.com

Printed in U.S.A.

CHAPTER ONE

EDEN was in the changing cubicle pinning up the hem on a customer's skirt when she heard the shop door open.

'You're always very busy,' the older woman commented. 'I suppose people just don't have the time to do their own alterations these days.'

'I'm not complaining.' With a rueful smile, Eden eased the last pin into place and rose upright. Five feet four inches tall and slightly built, she wore her thick golden hair twisted up into a clip. Her heart-shaped face was dominated by her clear green eyes.

Emerging from the cubicle, she looked in some surprise at the two men in business suits, who in company with a young woman were talking to her middle-aged assistant, Pam.

'These people are looking for you, Eden.' Pam could not hide her curiosity.

'How can I help you?' Eden asked.

'Eden James?' The older of the two men double-checked.

Conscious of the keen appraisal she was receiving from the trio and also of the indefinable tension they exuded, Eden nodded slowly.

'Is there somewhere we could talk in private, Miss James?'

Eden's eyes widened.

'Perhaps upstairs in your apartment,' the young woman suggested briskly.

She both looked and sounded like a police officer, Eden reflected, her anxiety increasing. But usually the police identified themselves first. Aware that her two employees and single customer were a captive audience, she flushed and hurriedly opened the door that led into the short passage which gave entrance back out onto the street.

'Could you tell me what this is about?' Eden prompted tautly then.

'We were trying to be discreet.' The older man now extended an official identity card for her inspection. 'I'm Superintendent Marshall and this young woman is Constable Leslie. This gentleman with me is Mr Rodney Russell, a special advisor from the Foreign Office. May we go upstairs to talk?'

Somehow, Eden found herself responding automatically to that calm note of command. What did they want? The police? A senior policeman too. The Foreign Office? *The Foreign Office?* Her mind blanked out with sudden horror and her hand started to shake as she stuck the key into the lock on her front door. Damiano! For so long, she had waited for such a visit but here it was catching her totally unprepared. When had she stopped fearing every phone call, every ring of the doorbell? *When?* Guilt-stricken dismay at that discovery about herself froze her to the spot.

'It's all right,' the female police officer asserted, contriving to gently urge Eden out of her paralysis and over the threshold. 'We haven't come here to break bad news, Mrs Braganzi.'

Mrs Braganzi? The name she had left behind when the cruel spotlight of press intrusion had become more than she'd been able to handle. So many reporters had wanted to ask her what it was like to be the wife of an important man who had simply disappeared into thin air. Refused those interviews, tabloid interest in Eden Braganzi had taken a nastier turn.

Not bad news? Eden blinked, mind briefly focusing again. How could it *not* be bad news after five years? There was no good news possible! And then natural common sense exercised its sway and steadied Eden a little. Was this yet another official courtesy call; was that it? Just letting her know that the case was still open but unsolved? It had been some time since anyone official had requested actual face-to-face contact with her. She herself had gone long past the stage where she continually phoned them, pushing, pressuring, finally hysterically begging for some action that she had only gradually come to appreciate they could not offer her. And only at that point had she begun finally to give up hope...

After all, Damiano's brother, Nuncio, and his sister, Cosetta, had given up hope of his survival within a month of his disappearance. Damiano had been in the South American republic of Montavia when a military coup had taken place. In the street violence which had followed in the capital city that day, Damiano had simply disappeared. He had checked out of his hotel and climbed into a limousine which should have taken him to the airport and his flight home. But that had been the last reliable sighting of him alive. The bodyguards in the car behind had been blown off the road by an explosion. Unhurt but with their vehicle wrecked, they had lost the limousine. Damiano and the limo and the driver had all vanished without trace.

During the subsequent enquiries, the new dictatorship had not been particularly helpful, but then by that time opposition to the coup had been spreading and a full-scale civil war had been threatening Montavia. The overstretched authorities had had little interest in the disappearance of a single foreign national and had pointed out that, during the fighting which had raged a full week in the city, many people had died or disappeared. There had been no trail to follow and no witnesses had come forward. But neither had there been any evidence found to actually *prove* that Damiano had been killed. It had been that appalling lack of proof of any kind which had tormented Eden for more years than she could bear.

'Please sit down, Mrs Braganzi,' some one of the three prompted her.

Didn't the police always ask a person to sit down when there was a nasty shock coming? Or was that only how actors portrayed the police in television productions? Still finding it impossible to concentrate, but slightly irritated at being ordered around in her own home, Eden sat down in an armchair and watched the two men settle themselves on the small couch opposite. The frown-line on her brow deepened. Their faces were taut, flushed, almost eager.

'Constable Leslie was telling you the truth, Mrs Braganzi. We're not here to break bad news but to give you extremely good news. Your husband is *alive*,' the police superintendent informed her with firm emphasis.

Frozen within the armchair, Eden stared at him in shaken disbelief. She parted dry lips. 'That's not possible...'

The other man, Russell, from the Foreign Office started to speak. He reminded her that at the outset of Damiano's disappearance a kidnapping had been suspected. But only along with every other possible crime or reason under the sun, Eden recalled, her dazed mind momentarily straying back five agonising years.

'After all, your husband was...*is*,' Russell corrected himself at speed and continued, 'a very wealthy, influential man in the international banking fraternity—'

'You said alive...' Eden broke in shakily, her face stricken as she surveyed the men in instinctive condemnation that they should dare to try to raise hopes she did not believe she could stand to have resurrected. 'How could Damiano still be alive after so many years? If he's alive, where has he been all this time? You've made a mistake...a dreadful, dreadful mistake!'

'Your husband is alive, Mrs Braganzi,' the superintendent spelt out with measured care and confidence. 'Naturally coming out of the blue as it has this is a considerable shock for you. But please believe what we are telling you. Your husband, Damiano Braganzi, is alive and well.'

Eden trembled, searching their faces and then suddenly shutting her eyes tight. She was struggling to overcome disbelief and simultaneously offering up a prayer of desperate hope to God. Let it be true, let it be real, please don't let me wake up if it's a dream—for over the years there had been many such dreams to torment her.

'Your husband surfaced in Brazil almost two days go,' the Foreign Office advisor divulged.

'Brazil...' Eden echoed shakily.

'He has spent over four years in prison in Montavia and on his release he had the good sense simply to slip quietly out of the country again.'

'P-prison?' Eyes shattered, Eden stared at the younger man with ever-mounting incredulity. 'Damiano's been in prison? How...*why*?'

On the day on which Damiano had disappeared, he had been kidnapped and taken to a military camp in the countryside. A military camp? She frowned at that unexpected information. A few days later, with civil war raging through the tiny republic, rebel forces had attacked the camp and in the ensuing battle Damiano had received serious head injuries. Finding a wounded prisoner in the aftermath, the rebels had quite naturally assumed that he was one of their own.

'Your husband is a fluent Spanish speaker. That and his quick thinking saved his life. He received treatment at a field hospital in the jungle. He was only just beginning to recover when he was picked up by the government soldiers, cleaning up the last pockets of resistance. He was imprisoned for being a member of the guerrilla forces.'

Damiano was alive...Damiano was *alive*! Eden was beginning to put faith in what she was being told although still every sense screamed at her to be cautious. She was fighting so hard to concentrate but she found that she just couldn't. She felt stupid, numb, disbelieving.

'Naturally you are wondering why your husband didn't immediately identify himself when he was captured,' the bland-faced Russell continued. 'He believed that admitting his true identity would be signing his own death warrant. He was aware that he had originally been kidnapped by soldiers loyal to the current dictatorship in Montavia. He knew that the kidnapping had been bungled and that, from that point, there had never been any intention of letting him go alive...'

Eden blinked, struggling to focus on the Foreign Office advisor and absorb what she was being told. Her blood was chilling in her veins, her tummy turning queasy. Damiano had been kidnapped, *hurt*... Her own worst imaginings had come true.

'Appreciating that his survival would be a severe embarrassment to the Montavian government, your husband decided that he would be safer retaining his assumed identity and accepting the prison term. On his release, he headed for the border with Brazil and from there to the home of a businessman called Ramon Alcoverro—'

'Ramon...' Eden whispered, slowly shaking her pounding head, lifting her hand to press her fingers against her damp, taut brow as if to aid her thinking powers. 'Damiano went to college with someone called Ramon.'

'About an hour from now, your husband will be landing on English soil again and he is keen that his homecoming should be kept from the media for as long as possible. For that reason, we have been discreet in our approach to you.'

Damiano alive, Damiano coming home. *Home?* To his family, of course, but *not* to her! In sudden, raw, shaken turmoil, Eden sat there, experiencing simultaneous joy and agony. These people had come here to make their announcement because she was still legally Damiano's wife and next of kin. But Eden was painfully aware that her marriage had virtually been over by the time of her husband's disappearance. Damiano had never loved her. He had married her on the rebound and lived to regret the impulse.

When had she forgotten that reality? When had she begun living in her own imagination? For Damiano would never return home to *her*. Had circumstances not cruelly intervened, he might well have come home to ask her for a divorce five years ago. Hadn't his own brother suggested that? And now, after the ordeal he had suffered, he would be anxious to get on with his life again. Indeed, in all likelihood, after hearing what had happened during his absence, Damiano would make no attempt to see her and any contact made would be through a divorce lawyer.

'Mrs Braganzi…Eden, may I call you Eden?' the superintendent enquired.

'His family…the Braganzi, his brother and his wife, his sister…' Eden framed dully. 'They must be overjoyed.'

The senior policeman's face stiffened. 'As far as I understand the somewhat limited information that I have received, your husband's family received a call from Ramon Alcoverro and immediately flew out to Brazil on their private jet.'

Eden froze at that disconcerting news, what colour remaining in her cheeks draining away to leave her deathly pale. Damiano's family had already flown out without even bothering to contact her and give her the news of his survival? She dropped her head, sick to the stomach at such cruelty.

'At times such as these, particularly where families have become estranged, people can act very much without thought,' the older man commented in the taut silence. 'We only became aware of the situation when the embassy in Brazil contacted the Foreign Office. They required certain information before they could issue a replacement passport to your husband so that he could travel home.'

Eden still said nothing. She was studying the carpet with eyes that ached. Nuncio had probably already told Damiano why he had not brought Eden out to Brazil with him. Those dreadful lies that had been printed about her in that newspaper only three months after Damiano had gone missing! The scurrilous gossip and opprobrium that had finally broken her spirit and forced her to leave the Braganzi home for the sake of her own sanity.

Rodney Russell took up the explanation in a brisk tone. 'By that stage, your husband was demanding to know why you had not been informed, unaware that his own family had failed to keep us up to date on developments.'

Eden blinked and looked up very slowly. 'Really?'

The superintendent gave her a soothing smile. 'I gather Damiano made it very clear that he can't wait to be reunited with his wife—'

Eden studied him with strained eyes of disconcertion. 'Damiano can't wait to see…me?' she whispered in faltering interruption, certain she must have misheard him.

'He's flying into Heathrow at noon and then he's taking a helicopter trip to an airfield just outside town. We'll convey you there. Obviously the hope is that it will be possible to evade any media attention.'

'He wishes to see *me*?' An almost hysterical little laugh escaped Eden's convulsed throat. She twisted her head away and lowered it, feeling the hot, stinging rush of tears hitting her eyes.

She wanted privacy but instead she had strangers watching her every reaction. Strangers who had to be well aware just what a charade her marriage had become by the time Damiano had gone missing. She ought to be used to that reality now, the knowledge that nothing had been too sacred to commit to an information file somewhere. But then the behaviour of Damiano's family in recent days spoke louder than any volume of words.

Nonetheless, after Damiano had vanished, there had
been a full-scale investigation by both the British and
the Italian authorities. Financial experts had gone in to
check that the Braganzi Bank was still sound. They had
looked for fraud or evidence of blackmail or secret ac-
counts. They had even looked for links between
Damiano and organised crime syndicates. Then they
had turned their attention to his own family circle to
see if anybody there might have employed a hitman to
get rid of him while he was abroad.

No stone had been left unturned. No opinion had
gone unsought. No question had been too personal or
too wounding to ask. Damiano had been too rich and
way too important to just disappear without causing
muddy ripples of suspicion to wash over everybody
connected with him. And nobody had suffered more
than Eden, the wife his snobbish siblings had secretly
despised, the wife who had swiftly become the target
of their collective grief and turmoil. Nuncio and his sister, Cosetta, had turned on Eden like starving rats on
prey. She had even been blamed for the fact that
Damiano had gone to Montavia in the first place.

'In situations such as this, we normally arrange spe-
cialist counselling and a period of protective isolation
for the victim,' Rodney Russell remarked, 'but your
husband has categorically refused that support.'

'I believe Damiano said he would prefer prison to
counselling,' the superintendent said with wry amusement.

A cup of tea was settled on the low coffee-table in
front of Eden. 'You've had a major shock,' the female
constable said kindly. 'But you're going to be reunited
with your husband this afternoon.'

At that staggering reminder, Eden rose in one jerky

motion and walked into her bedroom several feet away. She closed her eyes again, fighting for some semblance of composure. Damiano was alive; Damiano was on his way home. To *her*? She scolded herself for letting her thoughts slide once again in the wrong direction. A selfish direction. If Damiano wanted her now, she would be there for him. Naturally, obviously. In fact, if Damiano had asked for her, nothing would keep her from his side!

Had Nuncio kept quiet about her supposed affair, after all? Yet if he had, what excuse had he given Damiano for his failure to bring Eden out to Brazil with him? And what was Damiano likely to say when he came back? How was she to explain why she had left the Braganzi family home? Shed his name to hide behind another name? Built a new life far from what had so briefly been hers?

Struggling to suppress her mounting fears, Eden focused on the framed photo by her bed. Damiano smiling. All sleek, dark good looks and cool Italian charisma. It had been taken on their honeymoon in Sicily. But they had only been together seven months in total. Long enough though for her to see him withdraw from her, for her to stop expecting the connecting door between their bedrooms to open again, for him to start spending more and more time abroad on endless banking business. Long enough to break her heart. Love like that didn't go away. Love like that just *hurt*.

A light knock sounded on the ajar bedroom door. 'Are you all right?'

Mastering concerns which were pushing her close to panic at what should have been a most ecstatically happy moment, Eden turned a pale, tear-wet face to the young female officer. 'What now?'

'We'll leave for the airfield in half an hour. If I were you I'd shut up shop for the day and just think about what I wanted to wear.'

Wear? Eden swallowed a shaken laugh. Damiano... Damiano. What had he suffered? Kidnapped, his life threatened, seriously injured, locked up in some primitive foreign prison. Damiano, whose life had not prepared him in any way for such an ordeal. Damiano, born to wealth, command and supreme privilege. Once he had liked to see her in green. That thought just popped up out of nowhere and spawned a second, no less trivial recollection. Green had been his favourite colour.

She ransacked her wardrobe with suddenly frantic hands. Maybe he only wanted to see her to say, 'Hi, I'm back *but*...' without his precious family hanging around in the background. And Annabel, his first love, his true love. How could she have forgotten Annabel? Annabel Stavely, Damiano's ex-fiancée, who in the years since had had a child by a father she had refused to name but who remained single. Eden raised her hands to her face. Her hands were shaking, her palms cold and damp. She was a basket case with an out-of-control mind and the most desperate crazy desire to shout and scream with excitement and fear at one and the same time...

The phone rang barely a minute before Eden and her escort left the apartment.

'Eden?' It was Damiano's younger brother, Nuncio.

Shaken that her brother-in-law should finally call her after so many years of silence, Eden literally stopped breathing. She was instantly afraid that he was ringing as his brother's messenger to say that Damiano would not, after all, be flying on to see her and she whispered strickenly, 'Yes?'

'I have told Damiano nothing. How do I welcome him home with such news?' Nuncio demanded in a tone of bitter condemnation. 'I was forced to lie and say that we had lost contact with you after you moved out. But you had better tell him the truth for I will not stand by and see my brother made to look a fool by my silence!'

The truth? As Eden replaced the phone again with a trembling hand her own bitterness almost prompted her to pick it up again and call Nuncio back. But it was the temptation of a moment and swiftly set aside. In any case, he would never believe her, would he? Neither he nor anybody else would believe or indeed even *want* to believe the real truth, which was that her two best friends had betrayed her and ultimately left her to carry the can.

'You must understand that the man you remember *won't* be the man who will be coming home to you,' Rodney Russell informed her with daunting conviction as they sat in the back of the unmarked police car on the way to the airfield. 'It will be a great strain for both of you to rebuild your relationship—'

'Yes...of course.' Wishing he would stop winding her up with such warnings, Eden listened with veiled and ever more anxious eyes. The lecture about post-traumatic stress syndrome had been scary enough.

'Damiano is returning to a world he lost five years ago. It will be a challenge for him to adjust. He will suffer from mood swings, frustration and a sense of bitter injustice at the years that have been stolen from him. At times, he will crave solitude, but at other times he may relentlessly seek out company. He may be withdrawn, moody, silent or he may put on the macho-man act of the century but it won't *last*—'

'No?' she queried tautly.

'Try to appreciate that however your husband reacts now will not be a fair indication of how he'll be when he has come to terms with what has happened to him. This will be a transition period for Damiano.'

'Yes.' That last assurance had sent her heart sinking like a stone. She wasn't stupid. Was he warning her that Damiano might be seeking her right now but that in a few weeks he might walk away again? Did he think she fondly imagined that paradise might now be miraculously reclaimed from the debris of a marriage foundering five years ago? She was not so simple, nor so foolishly optimistic. She expected nothing, would ask for nothing from Damiano. She just wanted and desperately needed to *be* there for him. But she was challenged to believe that Damiano might need her. Damiano Braganzi had never been known to admit a need for anybody or anything.

It had been she who'd said, 'I love you,' but he had never said those words. Yet once he had said them to Annabel, hadn't he? Or at least he had had them etched on a beautiful gold necklace: 'All my love, Damiano.'

'I think some fresh air would do you good, Eden,' the superintendent cut into her increasingly frantic thoughts and she realized only then that the car had arrived at the airfield.

'Yes...yes, it would.' She slid out of the car and breathed in deep in an effort to steady herself. 'How much longer?'

'Maybe ten minutes...' The older man had no need to ask what she meant.

Ten minutes to wait after five years? She was such a

bag of nerves. She paced the Tarmac, ignoring the door open in welcome at the small passenger terminal. She smoothed trembling hands down over the fine green wool dress which was absurdly warm for a summer day but all that she still possessed in that colour.

'Russell is only doing his job as he sees it,' the senior policeman remarked quietly, 'but, accordingly to my sources, your husband is in remarkably good condition both physically and mentally.'

Eden nodded, a little of her tension ebbing, and then she heard a distant whirr. She jerked, throwing her head back to search the sky with fraught eyes. She saw a dark speck, watching it growing larger, her whole being centering on the helicopter as it came in to land. She still could not quite credit that Damiano was on that craft, that Damiano was about to emerge and walk across the Tarmac towards her.

In spite of everything she had been told, she was still terrified that somehow all these people and even his family had got it wrong and that the man who had turned up in Brazil wasn't really who they thought he was. An impostor—well, why not? Wasn't that at least possible? Mightn't somebody have boned up on Damiano's life and even had plastic surgery? Wouldn't it be worth a try to step into the shoes of so very rich a man? And wouldn't Nuncio, who had worshipped the ground his elder brother had walked on and who had been inconsolable when he'd gone missing, have been an easy and credulous target?

Rigid, she watched the helicopter settle down about a hundred feet away. A door thrust open. She trembled, cold and clammy with fear. And then she saw a very tall, very well-built male springing out, with long, powerful black-jean-clad legs, and also wearing a white

T-shirt and leather flying jacket. Black hair, far longer than she would have expected, blew back from his lean, hard-boned features. His skin was deeply bronzed. Her breath caught in her throat. She couldn't breathe. There was just this massive explosion of crazy joy inside her and she didn't notice herself moving forward at first hesitantly and then breaking into a run.

Damiano let her run to him. He just came to a halt about thirty feet from the helicopter. Later she would remember that, wonder about it. But at that instant she was all reaction and no thought. Every prayer answered, every fear for that moment forgotten, Eden just hurled herself at his big powerful frame, heart racing so fast she reeled dizzily against him as he closed his arms around her.

'You missed me, *cara*?' His rich, dark drawl wrapped round her, shutting out everything else as he bent his head down to her level.

Her face was squashed into his chest. He smelt so good, he smelt so familiar and she drank him in as if he were life-giving oxygen. 'Don't joke...*please* don't joke!' Eden sobbed into his shirt, clinging to him with both hands to stay upright.

CHAPTER TWO

FOR a couple of minutes, Damiano simply stood there holding Eden and she got the chance to get a partial grip on herself again and recall that they were in a public place.

'OK?' Damiano checked softly.

Eden breathed in shakily and lifted her head. 'I love you so much.'

She hadn't planned to say it, had not even thought of saying such a thing but the words came out in what felt like the most natural declaration in the world. She encountered eyes so dark and intent they were black. Unfathomable. A tiny spasm of fear tensed her muscles. Suddenly she became conscious of how rigid he was, how tight was the control he had over himself.

'And even after all this time, not a single doubt. I have to be the luckiest guy in the universe, *cara*,' Damiano responded with a roughened edge to his dark deep drawl, black eyes flashing gold as he scanned her anxious face, and then bent to sweep back up the travel bag he had set down. 'Come on, let's get rid of the welcome committee.'

He kept his arm round her narrow shoulders and walked her over to where the others hovered. Eden was still trembling, her mind in a tail-spin. She couldn't focus on what she had just said or his reaction. It was an effort to think far enough ahead to put one foot in front of the other and move. Yet on some subconscious level she sensed the difference in him but could not put a

21

label on what it was. Damiano had always been very controlled and very hard to read. He kept the volatile and expressive Italian side of his powerful personality under wraps. Except in bed.

That recollection made her cheeks burn and then slowly pale again. The luckiest guy in the universe? No, not in the bedroom with a wife he had once called the biggest prude in the western world! No, she had been a really dismal failure in that department, hampered by both her upbringing and her inhibitions, but most of all in the end by *his* dissatisfaction. For the more exasperated Damiano had become, the worse the problem had got. By then aware that everything she did and didn't do behind the bedroom door was under censorious appraisal, Eden had felt a shrinking reluctance she hadn't been able to hide from him. The pleasure he had given her had had a price tag attached and the cost had been too high for her pride to bear.

But when Damiano had gone missing, when she had had to face up to the appalling reality that he might be dead and might never come home to her again—oh, how she had beaten herself up for her failings then! In retrospect, her own hang-ups had begun to seem pathetic and selfish. Chewing at her lower lip, utterly dislocated from the dialogue which Damiano was coolly maintaining with what he had called the welcome committee, she focused on the long silver limousine pulling up with a surprised frown.

'The car's here. I don't want to hang around,' Damiano stated with a blunt lack of social pretence she had never heard him use before.

'Am I allowed to ask where you're heading, Mr Braganzi?' Rodney Russell enquired with the edged delivery of a male who, with the arrival of that chauffeur-driven car, had just been made to feel even more superfluous to requirements.

'Home...where else?' Damiano responded.

Home? Dear heaven, was he planning on having them driven straight back to London and yet another family welcome? A joyous celebration at which she would simply be the spectre at the feast?

'Where *is* home?' Damiano prompted with a rueful laugh as he strode towards the limousine. 'You had better give the driver directions.'

Her level of panic momentarily subsided at that clarification and she scolded herself for forgetting that, of course, he was already aware that she was no longer living in the vast Braganzi town house in London. However, he seemed to have taken that development in his stride. Having done as he requested, she climbed into the luxurious rear passenger seat. But the sense of panic swiftly returned to reclaim her. She had not thought beyond the moment of seeing Damiano again, indeed had barely attempted to even visualise what she could not imagine after so long. But now she felt like someone in a canoe without a paddle heading for the rapids.

'This feels weird to me too. Don't worry about it, *cara*,' Damiano breathed, reaching out without warning and closing his big hand over her tautly clenched fingers. 'No long-winded explanations of anything today. I'm back. You're here. That's all that matters at this moment in time.'

Eden stared at him. It seemed to be entirely the wrong time to be registering just how gorgeous he still was. The classic features, the superb bone-structure, the sensual curve to his perfectly modelled mouth. Damiano was stunningly good-looking but, unlike many such men, intensely masculine. Senses starved of him were already reacting to that unfortunate reality. The old familiar shame flooded her as she recognised the coil of heat in her belly, the swelling heaviness of her breasts beneath her clothing. Inwardly she cringed at how inappropriate and humiliating those responses were in the presence of a male who had rejected her outright on the one occasion she had plucked up the courage to invite him back to the marital bed. No, he definitely wasn't going to need her *that* way, she reminded herself, mortified by her own foolish susceptibility.

Once she'd got a hold on her embarrassing thoughts and tamped them firmly down again, her anxious eyes roved over his strong dark features and now marked the changes. His hard cheekbones might have been chiselled out of bronze and carried not an ounce of superfluous flesh. He was pale beneath that bronzed tan, his brilliant deep-set dark eyes shadowed with exhaustion. He would have had so much news to catch up on with his family that he probably hadn't slept on the flight back to England. In fact, he looked as if he hadn't slept in a week.

But there was an edge there now in that lean strong face that hadn't been there before. A tough, hard edge stamped like an overlay of steel on him. The smooth, sophisticated coolness she recalled had been replaced by a colder, deadlier quality. She had seen it in action with the welcome committee. There had been no apologetic pretence about his impatience to be gone. His accent had altered too. Five years of speaking Spanish and nothing else, no doubt carefully modelling his speech pattern on those around him. He was a very clever guy. He had not become the chairman of the Braganzi Bank by birth and precedent as his late father had. He had been voted in at the age of twenty-eight because he was quite simply brilliant at what he did.

The silence had become charged with an intensity she didn't understand. A slight frown-line indented her brow as she connected with his eyes. Eyes that now burned like golden flames. In a sudden movement, he meshed his other hand into her hair and brought her startled mouth up under his.

It was a shockingly intimate and shockingly unexpected sensual assault. Indeed, Eden, accustomed to the belief that her husband found her about as physically appealing as an ice bath, could not have been more stunned. The plunging eroticism of his tongue searching out the tender interior of her mouth shook her to her very depths and then sent such a current of scorching excitement through her that a strangled gasp was wrenched from her.

Instantly, Damiano released her, feverish colour scoring his cheekbones as he took a swift look at her shaken face, lowered his thick black lashes and breathed in a hoarse undertone, '*Mi dispiace*...I'm sorry, I can't think what came over me.'

Neither could Eden but most ironically she hadn't been about to complain. Her heart was banging as if she had run a three-minute mile. Her wretched body was tense and expectant; it had been so long since she had been touched in an intimate way. And she was hugely embarrassed because it was so obvious that Damiano regretted having kissed her. Lowering her head in self-protection, she chose to study their still-linked hands instead. Just grabbing was a sort of guy thing, she decided, trying to work out what had motivated Damiano, which was a challenge. After all, he had always confounded her understanding.

His hand tightened its grip on hers. 'Did I hurt you?'

'No...' So great was her self-consciousness, her response was a mere thread. Just grab me any time you like, she would have said to him had she had the nerve to credit that such an invitation would be welcome. But she didn't have the nerve and laboured under no such confidence-boosting belief in her own powers of attraction. Five years earlier, in a desperate attempt to save their marriage, she had tried to bridge the estrangement between them and failed miserably. Shortly before that disastrous trip to Montavia, Damiano had rejected her. He had said no to the offer of her body. What was more, he had said no with the kind of sarcasm which had cut her to the bone.

In the taut silence she brought her other hand round his and then, finally noticing the unfamiliar roughness there, turned his hand over and looked at it, for want of anything better to do. In complete bewilderment, she ran a fingertip over his scarred knuckles, his broken nails, and checked his palms. It was the hand of a man accustomed to hard and unrelenting manual labour.

'Challenge for the manicurist,' Damiano commented lazily.

'But...but how—?'

'I spent over three years working in a quarry six days a week. There wasn't much in the way of machinery—'

'A q-quarry?' Eden stammered, cradling his hand between both of hers with the most giant surge of shocked protectiveness surging up through her. A quarry? Damiano labouring in a quarry?

'After the first year, the military government awarded political status to all rebel prisoners. Good move. If you've banged up about a quarter of the entire male population and the country is so poor you can't afford to feed them, you have to prepare the footwork for an amnesty to let them out again,' Damiano explained levelly. 'And put them to work in the short-term so that they can produce enough not to be a burden on the economy.'

'A quarry...' Eden framed in shaken disbelief, emotion overpowering her even in the face of that deadpan recitation. 'Your poor hands...you had s-such beautiful hands—'

'*Dio mio*...I was *glad* to work! Beautiful hands?' Damiano countered with very masculine mockery. 'What am I? A male model or something?'

Squeezing her eyes tightly shut against the stinging tears already blinding her, Eden lifted his hand to her face and kissed his fingers. She couldn't have spoken or explained why to save her life, but she could no more have prevented herself from doing it than she could have stopped breathing.

In the aftermath of that gesture, the silence was so charged it just about screamed out loud.

Damiano withdrew his hand. Eden raised her face and clashed with stunned dark eyes and her face began to burn up like a bonfire.

'What's got into you?' Damiano demanded raggedly, his disconcertion over her emotional behaviour unconcealed.

'I'm...I'm sorry...' she mumbled, wishing a big hole would open up and swallow her, suddenly feeling so absolutely foolish.

'No...don't apologise for possibly the only spontaneous affection you have ever shown me!' Damiano urged, studying her with bemused intensity.

'That's not true,' she whispered in dismay at that

charge, uttered with such assurance as if it were a fact too well-known to be questioned.

But Damiano forestalled any further protest on her part by suddenly leaning forward to frown out at the suburban street the limo was now traversing to ask in honest bewilderment, 'Where on earth are we going?'

Eden tensed, 'My flat. It's on the outskirts of town—'

'You left our home to move into a *town* flat?' Damiano demanded in astonishment. 'I assumed that you had moved to Norfolk so that you could live in a country house!'

'It wasn't as simple as that, Damiano. For a start I wouldn't have had the money to buy myself a house and what would I have lived on? Air?' Eden heard herself respond with helpless defensiveness. 'The bank may have continued trading after your disappearance but all your personal assets were frozen which meant that I couldn't touch any of your money—'

'Naturally I am aware of that fact,' Damiano cut in drily. 'But are you seriously trying to tell me that my brother was not prepared to support you?'

It was amazing just how swiftly they had contrived to arrive at the very nub of the problem. The hard reality that Eden had become estranged from his family during his absence, news that would never, ever have gone down well with a male as family orientated as Damiano. And news which would go down even less well should he be told the truth of *why* the bad feeling had reached such a climax that she had no longer felt able to remain under the same roof.

'No, I'm not trying to tell you that,' Eden countered tightly, unable to bring her eyes to meet his in any direct way, playing for time while she attempted to come up with a credible explanation. 'I just felt that it was time I moved out and stood on my own feet—'

'After only four months? It did not take you long to give up all hope of my return!' Damiano condemned grittily.

The sudden silence reverberated.

And then Damiano made an equally abrupt and dismissive movement with one lean brown hand. 'No, forget that I said that! It was cruelly unfair. Nuncio himself admitted that he had believed me to be dead the first month and you never grew as close to my family as I had once hoped. The crisis of my disappearance divided you all rather than bringing you closer together—'

'Damiano,' Eden interceded tautly on the defensive.

'No, say no more. I would accept no excuses from Nuncio and I will accept none from you. That my brother should have flown out to Brazil *without* bringing my wife with him struck me as beyond the bounds of belief!' Damiano admitted grimly, his firm mouth hardening. 'Only nothing could have more clearly illustrated how deep the divisions between you had become—'

'Yes…but—'

'My disappointment at that reality was considerable but it is not something which I wish to discuss right now,' Damiano interrupted with all the crushing dismissal he could bring to any subject which annoyed him and which she well recalled from the distant past.

Eden had gone from shrinking terror at what might be revealed if she dared to protest her own innocence to instinctive resentment of that innately superior assurance. Dear heaven, did he think they were all foolish children to be scolded and set to rights on how they ought to be behaving? And then just when she was on the very brink of parting her lips and disabusing him of that illusion, it occurred to her that it would be wiser to let him think as he did for the present. Let sleeping dogs lie...only for how long would they lie quiet? Stifling that ennervating thought, Eden swallowed hard.

However, she need not have worried about where the conversation was going for at that point the limo drew up outside the narrow building where she both lived and worked. Damiano gazed out at the very ordinary street of mixed housing and shops with raised ebony brows.

'It may not be what you're used to but it's not as bad as it looks.' Eden took advantage of his silence to hurriedly climb out and lead the way, only to find herself hovering when Damiano paused to instruct the chauffeur in Italian. The limo pulled away from the kerb again and drove off.

Well aware that Damiano would not associate her with the name James etched in small print below the sign, 'Garment Alterations,' on the barred door, Eden hastened on past and mounted the steep stairs. The shop was shut. On Wednesday, most of the local shops took a half-day.

With a taut hand, she unlocked the door of her flat. Damiano strode in. In one all-encompassing and astonished glance he took in the compact living area and the three doors leading off to bathroom, bedroom and kitchen. 'I can't believe you left our home to live like this!'

'I wish you'd stop referring to the town house as *our* home. It may have been yours but it never felt like mine,' Eden heard herself respond, surprising herself with her own vehemence as much as she could see she had surprised him, for he had come to an arrested halt.

Damiano frowned. 'What are you talking about?'

'Living in the town house was like living in a commune—'

'A *commune*?'

'The communal Italian way of living; no matter how big the house is, there is never one corner you can call your own,' Eden extended jerkily.

'I was not aware that you felt like that about living with my family.' Damiano's outrage purred along every syllable of his response.

Eden knotted her trembling hands together. She was shaken by the strength of her desire to shout back at him for his refusal to accept the obvious and understand. That lack of privacy had contributed to their problems.

'Although I consider it beneath me to make the reminder, you came from a home no bigger than a rabbit hutch where I am quite sure it was an even bigger challenge to find a corner you could call your own,' Damiano framed with sardonic bite.

It was so crazy to be arguing about such a thing now. Her brain acknowledged that reality but, hurt that he should refer to the vast difference between their backgrounds, she could not keep her tongue still. 'So because you viewed our marriage as being along the lines of King Cophetua and the beggar maid—'

'King...who?'

'I was supposed to be *grateful* to find myself in a house that belonged to not just one but *two* other women!'

'What other women?' Having given up on establishing who the fabled King was, Damiano was studying her now as if she were slow-witted.

Eden's hands parted and then knotted into fists.

'Nuncio's wife, Valentina, and your sister, Cosetta. It was their home long before I came along—'

'I cannot believe we are having this absurd argument.'

'I couldn't even redecorate my own bedroom without offending someone…and you think I should have *liked* living like that? Always guests with us at meal times, always having to be polite and on my best behavior, never being able to relax, never being alone anywhere with you but in a bedroom—'

'And there least of all if you could help it,' Damiano slotted in reflectively. 'You would fall asleep in company before you would go upstairs at night. I *did* get the message.'

At that unanswerable reminder and assurance, Eden turned pale. The pained resentment went out of her then as if he had punched a button. She was both taken aback and embarrassed that she should have dragged up something which was so outstandingly trivial and inappropriate in the light of what *he* had endured since. And so great was that sense of shamed self-exposure, she just turned round jerkily and hurried off into the kitchen, muttering feverishly, 'You must want a coffee.'

She left behind her a silence, a huge silence.

With a trembling hand, she put on the kettle. 'Do you want anything to eat?'

'No, thanks,' Damiano countered. 'With Nuncio fussing round me like a mother hen, I was practically force-fed all the way from Brazil!'

He had followed her as far as the doorway. Out of the corner of her eye, she snaked a nervous glance at his enervating stillness. So tall, so dark, so heartbreakingly handsome. He was here, he was home—well, in her home temporarily. She loved this guy, she really,

really loved this guy. And here she was raving at him about stuff that was five years out of date and of about as much relevance to him now as an old weather report!

Was she out of her mind? It wasn't fair to hold his shock at the way she was living against him. He had left her behind in a mansion with twenty-five bedrooms and a full quota of domestic staff. Evidently, he had assumed that she would be protected by his brother's wealth from the usual financial problems of a wife with a husband who had vanished. So it was understandable that he should be astonished, even annoyed to find her ensconced in a tiny flat, existing on a budget that wouldn't have covered what his sister spent on shoes in a week.

'I didn't realize that you disliked living with my family...I never thought about that possibility,' Damiano admitted flatly.

'It's all right...I don't know why I mentioned it,' Eden gabbled in an apologetic surge, desperate to placate. 'It's so unimportant now—'

'No, it's not. I'll stay here until this evening *but*...'

Oh, dear heaven, he was going to leave her again! In a short space of time, it seemed she had alienated him, driven him off. A chill so deep it pierced her like a knife spread through Eden.

'I just need more space around me right now...OK?'

'OK...' Eden whispered so low she was almost drowned out by the boiling kettle. Space? Personal space and freedom, the sort of psychological stuff the Foreign Office advisor had tried to give her a crash course in understanding, she presumed, feeling sick. He wanted space away from her, he wanted to *escape* from her after less than a hour. She felt as if the roof were coming down on her, crushing the breath from her body.

'I've got twenty-four hours of meetings mapped out ahead of me already,' Damiano said levelly. 'There are legal niceties to be dealt with, press announcements to be made, new arrangements to be set in motion at the bank. I can't stay here. I *have* to be in London.'

He had never intended to stay. This had just been a flying visit. Literally! While he'd spoken, she had started to make the coffee on automatic pilot but as he continued to speak, and her heart sank, automatic pilot failed her. She didn't even notice that the cup she was filling was overflowing.

'*Porca miseria!*' Suddenly Damiano was right there behind her, his hands closing urgently over her taut shoulders as he yanked her back out of reach of the pool of boiling water about to cascade off the edge of the worktop. 'You almost scalded yourself!'

Pale and trembling, Eden focused on the hot water pouring down on to the floor with dismayed eyes.

'Just go and sit down...I'll deal with the flood,' Damiano asserted, thrusting her towards the door with determination. 'I think you're still in shock.'

From the sitting room Eden paused to look back and watch Damiano mopping up. 'It just doesn't seem real...you doing something domesticated like that, you being here,' she mumbled unevenly.

She encountered brilliant dark eyes as intent on her as she was on him. 'You're as white as a sheet, *cara*. Sit down.'

She sat because she was honestly afraid that, if she didn't, she might fall down. It seemed just a minute later but of course it must have been longer than that by the time Damiano reappeared and placed a cup of coffee in front of her. Damiano, who had once pressed a bell to get a cup of coffee or anything else he fancied. Yes, she thought in the disorientated manner of someone too strung up to reason rationally: Annabel would have come running back had Damiano so much as snapped his fingers. Even *after* he'd married! Struggling to get her wandering mind back under control, Eden fought for some semblance of composure.

'You're just coming apart at the seams...' Damiano groaned, bending over her without warning and lifting her up, only to lay her down again full length on the sofa. He snatched up the throw from the arm of one of the chairs and carefully arranged it over her. He hunkered down on a level with her, smoothed her hair back from her drawn face and breathed in a ragged undertone of regret. 'I've always been such a selfish bastard.'

The rawness of his emotions was etched in every line of his lean strong face. In the whole of their marriage, Damiano had never behaved as he just had or indeed looked or spoken as he did then. Eden was transfixed. Guilt...was this guilt she was hearing, guilt that he had hurt her? For she had made a hash of things within the first minute of seeing him again. Telling him she *loved* him! Dear heaven, where had her wits and her pride been? Five years on from a marriage he had long known to be a mistake! It was a wonder that he had even been prepared to give her these few hours. He was trying to let her down gently but equally impatient to get back to his own life. Back to the bank, back to the family from hell...

'I have had a long time to think about our marriage,' Damiano stated almost harshly.

'I know...' She shut her eyes because she just wanted to shut him up before he said more than she could stand to hear. She did not want the full spotlight of his attention on her. She just might break down and start sobbing and pleading.

'I was cruel...'

She jerked her chin in dumb acknowledgement and then whipped over on to her side, turning her narrow back to him, so much tormented emotion swilling about inside her, she was afraid she would break apart under the pressure. She crammed a fist against her wobbling mouth, willing herself into silence.

'I tried to make you into something you couldn't be...'

Sexy, adventurous, wanton, seductive. That was what he had wanted. That was what he hadn't got. The sort of female who pranced about in front of him in silk underwear and was willing to have sex somewhere other than in a bed with all the lights switched off. The sort of female who played a more active part, who did something more than simply *lie* there. The sort of female who was able to *show* him that she wanted him.

'I had unrealistic expectations,' Damiano breathed in a driven admission.

Formed by a vast experience of other women to who such outdated inhibitions had evidently been unknown, she reflected with a bitter sense of squirming failure.

'I wasn't used to hearing that word, "no"...'

Well, he had certainly heard it a lot both before *and* after he'd married. Would it really have killed her to take her clothes off in front of him or let him undress her just once? Couldn't she have said, 'yes' that time he had started kissing her in the car when he had come back from a long business trip?

'What I'm trying to say is that I was wrong to make the bedroom such an issue...do you think you could say something?' Damiano murmured tautly.

'Nothing to say,' Eden whispered, keeping her back turned to him, tears running down her cheeks.

The silence fizzed like the shaken bottle of a soft drink, threatening explosion from pent-up pressure. She had done the wrong thing again. He wanted her to talk but what on earth did he expect her to say? Everything he had said meant just one thing to Eden: he wanted a divorce, a civilised one where blame was shared and platitudes were mouthed and nobody held spite. So he was smoothing over the past, trying to change it. What else could he be doing when he said he should not have made the bedroom such an issue?

For wasn't sexual satisfaction of major importance to most men? And, to a male of Damiano's ilk, a taken-for-granted expectation. After years of being pursued, flattered and treated to every feminine wile available, a rich and powerful man took it as his due that he would marry a sensual woman. But then she knew *why* Damiano had ended up asking someone as unsuitable as she had been to marry him, didn't she? Her tummy turned over. On the rebound from Annabel, he had been a male used to winning every time, and had been challenged by Eden's refusal to sleep with him.

'I've got some calls to make,' Damiano said flatly.

'I'm sorry, I—?'

'No!' Damiano countered with grim disapproval. 'I do not want to hear you always apologising. You weren't like that when I married you…I *made* you that way by acting like a bully!'

So taken aback was Eden by that declaration that she opened her eyes and lifted her head with a jerk, but the only reward she received was the decisive snap of the bedroom door closing. A bully? Was that how she had made him feel with her inability to talk or respond on the level he required? That idea pained her even more and sent her thoughts winging back into the distant past...

Her parents had married late in life and she had been an only child, her father the gamekeeper on a remote Scottish estate. One of her earliest memories was the hum of the sewing machine for her mother had been a gifted seamstress whose talents had brought in much-needed extra income. Hard work had been respected and idle chatter discouraged in a household in which emotions had been kept private and demonstrative affection had been rare.

By the time that Eden had gained her teaching qualification at college, her mother had died and her father had asked her to return home to live. When the sole teacher in the tiny local school had taken maternity leave, Eden had been engaged to fill the temporary vacancy. Over the years, the Falcarragh estate on which she had been born had changed hands many times. Having gone out of private ownership, it had been traded just like a business investment and had long been run by a London-based management team of executives, who had rarely visited but who had excelled at cutting costs.

Even though she had by then been twenty-one, love and its attendant excitements had played little part in Eden's life. The estate manager's son, Mark Anstey, her childhood playmate, had remained her closest friend. As a teenager, however, she had had a major crush on Mark. She had only outgrown it when she'd realised that although she'd been very fond of him, she just hadn't been able to imagine kissing him. Mark had felt more like the brother she had never had.

Damiano had stridden into Eden's life that same win-

ter when his car had gone off the road in the snow. Her
father had been away from home, staying with his
brother who had been ill. The adverse weather had
closed the school early the day before. The following
evening, Eden had been astonished when the dogs had
started barking to warn her of a visitor for, with blizzard
conditions, threatening outside, all sensible people had
been safe indoors.

Answering the door, she'd stared in initial dismay at
the very tall and powerfully intimidating figure which
Damiano had cut in a snow-encrusted black coat.

'Mi dispiace,' he stated hoarsely, frowning with the
effort concentration took. 'But I need...I need the
phone.'

Registering only that he was feverishly flushed,
swaying on his feet and showing the confusion brought
on by being frozen, Eden stopped being intimidated at
speed. If he collapsed, she knew she wouldn't be capable of lifting so big a man. With innate practicality,
she closed her hand over his sleeve and urged him over
the threshold. 'Come in at once...'

She guided him towards the warmth of the hearth but
not too close to the heat. 'Phone...*per favore*,' he said
again, his dark-timbred drawl accented, the words
slightly slurred, but it was still a remarkably attractive
voice.

Stretching up on tiptoe, Eden instead began to remove the very heavy and sodden coat he wore, forcing
him to release the travel bag he still clutched as if his
life depended on it. Finding the jacket of the business
suit he wore beneath damp, she scurried round him to
unbutton it and ease him out of that as well. Damiano,
silent for possibly the only time in their entire acquain-
tance, stood there registering complete bewilderment at

what she was doing and blinking lashes long as black silk fans. *'Signóra?'*

'You must have a death wish,' she groaned out loud. 'Such unsuitable clothing for this weather—'

She hauled a blanket out of the chest by the wall and tried to reach up high enough to drape it round his shoulders, finally surrendering and planting a hand to his broad chest in an effort to persuade him down into the armchair behind him.

'Small...angel?' he queried, gazing down at her with bemused fascination, dark as midnight eyes lingering on her delicate features as he clumsily pinned her hand in place with ice-cold fingers. 'No rings...single?'

'Sit down,' Eden told him, hurriedly pulling her hand free.

He sank down heavily into the chair but continued to stare at her.

Eden arranged the blanket round him and then crouched down at his feet to remove his wet shoes and socks as quickly as she could, continuing to talk for fear that he might still lapse into unconsciousness. 'What's your name?'

'Damiano...'

She looked up and focused properly on his features for the first time since his arrival. She stilled, her absorbed gaze roving slowly over that startlingly handsome lean, dark face, her breath tripping in her throat. Even wet, he was just so incredibly good-looking. Gorgeous bone-structure, incredible eyes.

'Damiano,' she repeated shakily.

He gave her a sleepy but charismatic smile that rocked her heart on its axis and said something else in his own language.

With extreme effort she dragged her attention from

him and unzipped his travel bag in search of warm dry clothing. She extracted a pair of khaki jeans and an oatmeal sweater, the quality of both attracting her notice but not to the extent they should have done for she had little knowledge of designer labels. Was he a tourist? He was hardly dressed for the winter sports season. The coat and the suit were of the type a city businessman would wear to a formal meeting.

'You get changed while I'm heating up some soup for you,' she instructed him in an authoritative voice, the one she used with the rebellious older boys in her classroom. 'Don't you dare go to sleep on me!'

But even as she walked into the small scullery her heart was hammering so hard, she had to snatch in a sustaining breath and she could not resist the urge to glance back over her shoulder at him and look again.

She collided with beautiful dark deep-set eyes that made her feel dizzy and brainless for the first time in her extremely sensible life. 'You *do* look an angel...' he told her stubbornly.

'That's enough,' she tried to say briskly.

'No, it's only a beginning.'

And so it was. But, unfortunately, a beginning for two people without the slightest thing in common. Damiano soon recovered from that rare vulnerability which she found so very appealing. Having already discovered to his cost at the roadside that the reception was too poor in the area for his mobile phone to work, he was amazed when she let drop that her father had only got the landline phone connected the previous year and that the same problem with bad reception had prevented them from ever owning a television.

He was even more astonished that she didn't own a car. Yet he himself had climbed the steep-rutted track which ran over a mile down to the road and only a four-wheel drive could traverse it in bad weather. With her father away and the estate vehicle he utilised only insured for his use, Eden had been without transport. To get to school that week, she had been walking down to the road and catching a lift with one of her pupil's parents.

After eating, Damiano again requested the use of the phone and, since she naturally gave him privacy to make that call, she didn't pick up any hint of *who* he actually was. Mightn't she have drawn back and protected herself that night had she known how wealthy and powerful a male she had brought in out of the storm?

Indeed, although he later carelessly dismissed her claim as utterly ridiculous, Eden remained convinced that Damiano had *deliberately* avoided telling her that he owned the Falcarragh estate. In addition, he had not mentioned the Braganzi Bank or, for that matter, any facet of his high-powered lifestyle which might have alerted her to his true status. He had been content to allow her to believe that he was merely one of the salaried London executives involved in the running of the estate. Why, she had never understood, unless it had simply amused him.

By the time she showed Damiano into her father's bedroom, for he had no option other than to spend the night, she had talked herself hoarse. He had dragged the unremarkable story of her life out of her with a determination that only an ill-mannered response could have forestalled. And she had been flattered and fascinated by the heady effect of his powerful personality, megawatt charm and stunning good looks all focused exclusively on her.

The next morning, after the snowplough had been through, he insisted on making his own way down to the road to be picked up, but before he departed he asked her to have dinner with him that night and she agreed; of course she did. She suppressed the awareness that her father would disapprove of her dating a male he would regard as one of the 'bosses'. Rain came on that afternoon and Damiano arrived at the door in one of the estate four-wheel drives.

He had taken a room in the only local hotel and was critical of the meal they received in the cosy bar. Naturally. While she saw nothing wrong with anything they were served, the meal could hardly have been of the standard to which Damiano was accustomed. It was like a dream date for Eden to be seen out with a male whom other women couldn't take their eyes off. She adored his good manners, hung on his every witty word of conversation and marvelled at his ability to reach for her hand and hold it as if it was the most natural thing in the world.

And then, on the drive home, her dream bubble burst. 'I would have asked you to stay the night with me at the hotel but I imagine that the local teacher has to be careful of her reputation in a rural area like this,' Damiano remarked with incredible cool. 'It's fortunate that you don't have neighbours.'

He had known her for precisely twenty-nine hours and *already* he was expecting her to sleep with him! Eden was shocked out of her enchanted cloud of romance, embarrassed and then angry with him for wrecking everything and angry with herself for having foolishly expected more of him. With the exception of his singularly smooth and sophisticated approach, it seemed that, after all, Damiano was little different from the college students who had hassled her with crude pick-up lines and horribly blunt sexual invitations.

'I have no intention of letting you stay the night,' Eden breathed curtly.

'That was a negative,' Damiano mused with indolent, even amused unconcern. 'I'm gifted at changing negatives into positives.'

Tears burned the back of her eyes but rage gathered inside her. 'That kind of behaviour isn't part of my life and it never will be—'

'You're planning to become a nun?' Damiano incised with lashings of mockery, quite undaunted by her attitude. 'Let me tell you something about Italian men...we're extremely persistent when we want something—'

'I do not want to discuss this!' Eden interrupted in growing mortification. 'Just drop the subject—'

'I'm an upfront guy, *cara*. And, at my age, I cannot imagine having a relationship without sex—'

'Well, I'm not planning on having a physical relationship with anybody until I get married!' Eden shot back at him between gritted teeth.

Damiano was so shattered by that accidental admission which he had provoked her into making that he shot the car to a mud-churning halt outside her home and turned to scrutinise her with openly incredulous eyes. 'You're kidding me?'

Releasing her seat belt, as desperate now to escape him as she had been to *be* with him earlier in the evening, Eden scrambled out of the car. 'Goodnight!'

Damiano sprang out of the driver's seat and intercepted her before she could reach the door. 'You're still a virgin?'

Nobody had ever spoken that word to Eden's hot face

before and she could think of nobody she could have wanted to hear it from less. He said it in the same tone of disbelief which some people reserved for UFOs.

'Urgent re-think...possibly the concept of enjoying out mutual passion tonight was slightly premature,' Damiano groaned with unashamed regret.

Eden was hauling her keys out of her bag with a shaking and desperate hand. If she had had wings, she would have spread them and flown away. Sex had never been mentioned in her home, nothing so intimate ever discussed. Apart from frequent references to the social and moral consequences of casual intimacy, sex had been no more prevalent a subject in the city vicarage where she had boarded with her uncle's family while at college. 'Please shut up,' she gasped.

'I'm trying to understand what's going on here—'

'I made it quite clear—'

'But you're surely *not* expecting me to propose marriage to get you into bed?' Damiano persisted with sardonic cool.

And reacting to that wounding sarcasm, she slapped him. Without thinking about it, without meaning to do it, she just lifted her hand and slapped him across one high, hard cheekbone.

'You—'

'I'm sorry but—'

Damiano surveyed her with outraged eyes that turned gold in anger and pulled her to him with powerful hands to crush her startled mouth under his with an explosive passion that just blew her away.

Releasing her again, Damiano studied her shocked face and the hectic flush he had fired in her cheeks and suddenly, without the slightest warning, he laughed with genuine amusement. 'Some day soon, I swear you're going to be begging me for that, *cara mia*. I can wait for the day.'

CHAPTER THREE

EMERGING from that emotive trip back more than five years into the past, Eden listened to the distinct tones of Damiano's cultured drawl as he talked on the phone in her bedroom and slowly breathed in deeply.

Hadn't his own sardonic question come true in the end? He *had* married her to get her into his bed and, understandably, having gone to such lengths and practised such patience, Damiano had expected a wildly sensual wedding night and an orgy of a honeymoon. Only that hadn't come off either, Eden recalled, wretched tears gathering again as she stuck her face in a cushion.

'I'm going to try and catch a couple of hours of sleep before I fold. I'm so tired, I feel like I'm only half conscious,' Damiano admitted heavily from the bedroom doorway. 'Do you want me to use the sofa?'

It was the last straw. He'd come back after *five* years and was offering to sleep on a sofa that was only four-foot long, even though there was a double bed in her bedroom and he had to have noticed it!

'Please use the bed,' Eden squeezed out, will-power keeping a tremulous wail of self-pity from escaping.

'The limo will be here at seven to ferry me back out to the airfield. Wake me up in time,' he urged.

It's over, she tried to tell herself with accepting fatalism. It never worked. Just be grateful he's alive. But it wasn't enough—by no stretch of the imagination was it enough to compensate her for the devastating effect of Damiano walking back into her life like the ultimate

47

fantasy and then walking back *out* again. Here she was
curled up like a hedgehog hiding from him. More or
less business as usual, then? Here she was demonstrat-
ing all over again the kind of lie-down-and-die passivity
that drove Damiano clean up the walls!

Was this *all* she was capable of doing? Acting like a
helpless victim who had no influence over her own mis-
fortunes? How come she had just fallen straight back
into that old bad pattern of behaviour when she had
changed so much during his absence?

For she *had* changed, had had no choice but to become stronger and braver after what she had experienced. When Damiano had mentioned leaving again,
shock had settled over her like a blinding, suffocating
blanket. She had just shrunk in stature down to the level
of a carpet fibre, all fight, all confidence, all strength
leeched back out of her again as her worst fears came
true.

So are you just planning to let go without an argument?

Eden unfurled herself and stood up. The bedroom
door was slightly ajar. For how long had she been lost
in her own thoughts? She pushed open the door an inch
at a time, her heart thundering at the base of her dry
throat. Damiano was fast asleep in her bed, his glossy
black hair and his bronzed skin in stark contrast to the
pale bed linen. He was lying on his stomach, the duvet
tangled round his narrow hips, his powerful shoulders,
muscular arms and the long, spectacular golden sweep
of his back exposed. He was a riveting sight. Totally
male, totally breathtaking.

How often had she sneaked a look at Damiano half
naked? Her cheeks burned. Strange, wasn't it, that she
should have personally taken advantage of what she had

consistently denied him? But hadn't she always secretly enjoyed looking at him? Hadn't a single glimpse of Damiano just with his shirt off thrilled her to death? But she hadn't ever admitted that even to herself until now. The way she had been brought up such a sexual thought would have been considered shameless and not how a good and decent woman would think.

So she had been raised in a repressed and puritanical home with parents who had been heading for their sixties by the time she'd entered her teens. Why had she taken all that baggage with her into her marriage? Why hadn't she tried to shake free of her inhibitions just a little? Well, the truth was, she was very stubborn and very proud. And so was Damiano. Neither one of them had been prepared to compromise.

That time she had offered herself and he had rejected her, what had she said?

'I want a baby…'

Damiano had studied her with chilling dark eyes. 'You just put a double lock on your own chastity belt. That has to be the least tempting proposition any woman ever offered me. When you want *me* and when you can prove that on my terms, I might consider coming back to your bed.'

Was it too late now? For Damiano had had to go missing before she'd been able to understand *why* he had been so angry with her that day. Eden's hands curled into fists over her own past stupidity. The face-saving excuse of wanting a baby had been a huge mistake. Then he hadn't appreciated just how desperate she had been or how she had naively believed that getting pregnant might have kept him with her.

She walked back out of the bedroom and into the kitchen. There was a bottle of vodka in the cupboard.

Pam had given it to her for Christmas four years back, not then aware that Eden never touched alcohol. Yet another thing that had irritated Damiano: a bride who wouldn't even touch champagne at her own wedding! But she needed Dutch courage before she could do what she *had* to do, didn't she?

She poured herself a glass of vodka liberally combined with orange juice. Suppose he said no and fought her off? She would have to sort of creep up on him while he slept, not give him the chance to object. He had grabbed her and kissed her in the limo, hadn't he? For a split second, it had been as if he'd been unable to keep his hands of her! There surely hadn't been any women in that South American quarry and she had married a very highly sexed male. Turned him off it to the extent that she had actually started fearing that he might be obtaining what he no longer appeared to want at home *elsewhere*...

But, prior to his disappearance, Damiano had given her no cause to believe that he was being unfaithful, she reminded herself urgently. Now she had this one last chance. Maybe she had run out of chances. But he was worth the effort. She tiptoed back to the bedroom doorway and feasted her fraught eyes upon him. Oh, yes, he was still worth a major effort and in just a few hours he would be gone for ever!

Wrinkling her nose, she up-ended the glass and drank deep. Then she stripped off her clothes. She put on perfume, made careful use of her small stock of cosmetics and fussed endlessly with the blonde hair that tumbled round her shoulders in no particular style. As she usually wore her hair up, she had got lazy about getting it cut. She wondered if old vodka went off in strength and decided she had better drink some more. She was going to be everything Damiano had ever wanted just once. *Not* that prude he had left on the sofa. To prove that to herself, she walked naked out to the hall storage cupboard to dig out a box of keepsakes she had chosen not to leave behind in the town house.

Damiano had sent her a box of gorgeous silk lingerie the day before their wedding. The upfront guy spelling out his expectations, fantasies, hopes. No doubt, he had not appreciated just how outright intimidated she had been by that gesture or how deeply shocked her late father had been by the sight of such an intimate gift, for naturally the older man had demanded to know what had been in that wretched box and she had just cringed.

Eden slid into whisper-thin lilac panties and a matching low-cut bra. Better than being naked, she decided, bracing herself. She was beginning to feel a little strange…kind of skittish, enervated, gripped by the most ridiculous desire to dance. Damiano wasn't going to know what had hit him, she told herself, psyching herself up into her new and more adventurous persona.

Damiano was now lying on his back in a diagonal sprawl across the divan. Late afternoon sunshine was filtering through the thin cotton curtains at the window. From the foot of the bed, she eased up into the space left by the wall. She studied Damiano. The piratical dark stubble accentuating his strong jawline and beautifully moulded mouth, the riot of dark, curling hair hazing his powerful pectorals, the smooth golden skin wrapped round his sleek, strong muscles.

Just the thought of touching him made her tingle. Awkwardly, she edged further up the bed, ludicrously fearful of awakening him. She bent over him, mesmerised by the slow rise and fall of his chest, the soft rush of his breathing and finally by the vibrance of him even asleep. She lifted her hand and rested her fingers very lightly on his arm. He shifted, muscles flexing beneath her hand. She tensed but the need to express how much she loved him in the only way that seemed left was more powerful.

Lowering her head, Eden pressed her lips to his taut, flat stomach and ran the tip of her tongue over his skin. The taste of him made her shiver. Heat flooded her own trembling body, stirring her breasts, pinching her nipples into straining buds. The scent of him was an unbelievable aphrodisiac to senses starved for so long. Her hand settled to a powerful male thigh to balance herself and, breathing in deep, she began to ease back the sheet.

But with a slumbrous growl, Damiano shifted, startling her. He laced his fingers into her hair to draw her up to him. Eden had barely grasped that he was wakening and that control was no longer hers before he had claimed her mouth in a devouring and hungry kiss. Raw need raced through every fibre of her shaken body in response. Settling strong hands to her waist, he lifted her over him, long fingers splaying to her slender hips to urge her into potent contact with the virile force of his arousal.

The heat he ignited fired an almost painful ache deep in her pelvis. Eden quivered, a helpless moan of reaction escaping her. Almost instantaneously, Damiano stilled. His hands whipping up to her forearms, he held her back from him.

Stunned dark as night eyes clashed with hers. 'Eden?' he faltered in apparent disbelief. *'Che cos' hai?'*

It was one of those ghastly moments when time hung still and she would have done anything to move it on. As she registered that Damiano had automatically responded to her caresses before he was even properly awake, a burning tide of red skimmed up her throat to scorch her discomfited face. She watched in a state of stricken paralysis as his attention zeroed in on the scanty bra and brief set she wore. He blinked. Then he looked again with the kind of fixed attention which only accentuated his shock.

'*Per amor di Dio*...what on earth are you playing at?'

Prior to getting into the bed, Eden had nourished a comforting vision of Damiano waking up to snatch her to him with keen hands and mercifully silent enthusiasm. Instead, Damiano had pulled back from her to reassert control and was now asking what had to be the craziest question he had ever asked her.

'And why are you dressed like that?' Damiano enunciated with a level of incredulity which only seemed to be increasing with every second that passed. He now focused on the high-heeled shoes which she had put on and kept on.

'I...I don't know what you expect me to say...' Her admission emerged hopelessly slurred, the words tumbling together, provoking an even deeper frown between Damiano's winged ebony brows.

'Have you been drinking?' Damiano questioned rawly.

'Well, er...a bit—'

'*So*...' Damiano framed in a wrathful, low-pitched growl, black eyes blazing to gold as he scanned her guilt-stricken face. 'You had to hit the bottle to get back into bed with me?'

'Yes... I mean *no*!' she gasped, floundering in dismay and confusion at the anger he was revealing.

'*So* drunk you get into bed with your shoes on,' Damiano said thickly, fabulous bone-structure rigid as he swept her from him and dumped her back down on the mattress. 'I left behind a shy, uptight wife and now you're coming on to me tarted up like some high-class hooker!'

Aghast at that condemnation and utterly at a loss in the situation developing, Eden began to crawl backwards off the bed. 'No…no, it's not like that—'

'So *who* was it?' Damiano shot at her, his lean, dark features flushed with black fury, his dark drawl fracturing, long fingers snapping like handcuffs round her wrist before she could get out of reach. 'Who was it who worked this miraculous transformation while I was away? Don't you think I have the right to know who's been sleeping with my wife when I couldn't do anything about it?'

Her feverish colour had now ebbed to leave her pale. She stared back at him with shocked eyes. The savage tension churning up the atmosphere tore cruelly at her already frayed nerves. Damiano snatched in a starkly audible breath, lashes lowering on his smouldering gaze as he abruptly released her from his hold.

Eden scrambled off the bed and snatched up the dressing gown lying on the chair, pulling it on with shaking hands. 'Like some high-class hooker?' Was that how she had seemed to him? Mortification and shame churned up her stomach. He didn't want her…why had she imagined he would? Why had she got the crazy idea that five years on she might make good where she had failed before? Too little, too late. And now, thanks to her own foolishness, a nightmare seemed to be erupting around her: Damiano was already accusing her of having slept with some other man.

'Mark, I suppose…' Damiano gritted unevenly, his

hands curling into fierce fists. 'Sneaking, smooth little jerk just waiting his chance!'

For a split second Eden froze and then she backed out the door and fled into the bathroom. She thrust home the bolt on the door. So panicked by that final comment she could barely get air back into her lungs, she fought to get a hold of herself again. Did Damiano *know*, after all? Why else would he have mentioned Mark? Had someone already told him about those filthy lies printed about her by the tabloid press within months of his disappearance? What else was she supposed to think? Why else would he be thinking such a thing of her?

Damiano tried the handle. He rapped on the door. 'Open up, Eden. I've calmed down and we have to talk.'

But Eden retreated from the door and stared at the barrier, imagining herself growing old and grey behind it. Her brain felt like mush. She couldn't cope with this right now, couldn't cope with Damiano. Shedding the dressing gown, she tore off the scanty bra and briefs and thrust them into the waste bin with a shudder of chagrin. She kicked off the shoes and hauled on the dressing gown again, her face stiff with distress. Everything had gone horribly wrong; everything always seemed to go horribly wrong for her with Damiano.

'Eden...I'm going to break down this door if you don't come out.'

But she *knew* he wouldn't do anything like that. It wouldn't be cool. But then there had been nothing cool about the manner in which those accusations had come flying out of nowhere at her. 'You're leaving me anyway. Why am I letting you upset me? I'm not coming out!' she sobbed with sudden ferocious bitterness.

With a thunderous crash the door smashed open and banged off the wall behind it. Her compressed lips fell

open in shock. Pale as parchment, she surveyed
Damiano. He had pulled on his jeans but, bare-chested
and in need of a shave, his black hair tousled and his
brilliant eyes shimmering like starlight, he was an intimidating sight.

'Relax...' he urged in an evident attempt to soothe
her.

Eden was closer to collapse than relaxation. She
stared back at him with huge, shaken eyes. He had lost
his temper with her. He had smashed open the door
without hesitation. For that split second in her bewilderment at such unfamiliar behaviour, she was incapa-
ble of response.

Damiano strode forward and just reached for her. He
pulled her unresisting body close. His own heart was
hammering as fast as her own. He urged her back into
the sitting room. Her legs felt as weak as cotton wool
beneath her. She was shaking like a leaf.

'Why are you accusing me of leaving you?' Damiano
chided, evidently not having taken that accusation seriously. 'Why can't you just fly back to London *with*
me? It will only be for a couple of days. As soon as I
get these meetings over with, we're flying out to Italy.'

'Italy?' Finally, it dawned on Eden that she had misunderstood his intentions earlier. He might be leaving
her apartment but he was not planning to leave her behind as well. Sheer relief washed over her in such a
gigantic wave that she felt dizzy.

'One of the first things my brother told me was that
Nonna died over four years ago.'

Eden was appalled to appreciate that she had forgot-
ten that that news would greet Damiano on his return.
Old news to everybody else but *not* to him. When
Damiano had gone missing, his grandmother had been

devastated. Stress had undoubtedly contributed to the heart attack which had killed her and Damiano had to know that, Eden conceded painfully, for Damiano was no fool.

'I gather *Nonna* was in the midst of yet another grand restoration project at the time.' Repressed emotion roughened Damiano's vowel sounds and she swallowed hard on the thickness in her own throat. 'In her will, she specified that the Villa Pavone should be completed and maintained until I had been legally presumed dead. Since that fact is not generally known, I hope this Tuscan *palazzo* will supply us with a peaceful bolt-hole free from the attentions of the paparazzi.'

Finally daring to accept that Damiano intended them to stay together in the immediate future at least, Eden slowly released her pent-up breath, her worst fear now banished.

Damiano curved long, sure fingers below her chin and turned up her face, dark, deep-set eyes demanding that she stop evading his gaze. 'I shouldn't have pitched that stuff at you in the bedroom,' he asserted with cool clarity. 'You believed I was never coming back. You thought I was dead. I haven't got the right to interrogate you about the past five years. Rationally, I *know* that. But for a few minutes, waking up as I did, I over-reacted—'

'But I went on feeling married… I went on thinking about you even though you weren't there,' Eden protested with urgent tautness.

'*Sì*…I checked the dust pattern below the photograph of me by the bed,' Damiano said with a wry self-mockery that just tore at her heart. 'I know you didn't just drag it out of the closet for show today.'

Tears lashed the back of her eyes as she thought of

him checking in such a way. 'You mentioned Mark,' she reminded him tremulously, dropping her head again, still metaphorically waiting for the axe to fall.

'I'm afraid I never did warm to your childhood play-mate.' Damiano shrugged as if to stress how trivial he considered that former response on his own part. Yet Eden was surprised for she had never realised that he disliked the younger man. Indeed, at her request, more than five years earlier, Damiano had hired the younger man to help manage the Braganzi country estate outside Oxford. However, by the time a tabloid photographer had taken a covert picture of Mark passionately em-bracing a small slim blonde woman, Mark had actually been working out his notice for the Braganzi family. The estate had been joint-owned by the brothers. Nuncio, challenged by the prospect of maintaining the same high-rolling lifestyle without Damiano's assis-tance, had sold it.

But Damiano definitely didn't know about her sup-posed affair with Mark, Eden registered with heady re-lief. He couldn't *know* and still refer to Mark in that dismissive tone of disinterest. Furthermore, Damiano was taking her to Italy with him. This was not the time to start making awkward confessions and explanations, was it? Most particularly when she herself was innocent of any wrongdoing. Why dredge up all that nonsense now? Of course, she would raise the thorny subject some time with him, but at that moment all Eden wanted to concentrate on was holding onto her long-lost husband by any means within her power.

'Damiano…there hasn't been anybody else—'

'I don't need you to say that just for the sake of it. I'm not asking.' His sculpted cheekbones might have been carved from bronze as he made that assurance.

'But I'm telling you all the same.' Eden gazed up at him with clear eyes. 'Just for the record, there *hasn't* been.'

Damiano studied her with glittering intensity. 'If that's true, what was that astonishing seduction scene all about?'

Finally Eden grasped why he doubted her plea of innocence. Hot pink flooded her complexion. Her own unusually bold behaviour in the bedroom had roused his suspicions and brought on the very accusations which she had most feared!

'I know I made a mess of it,' she muttered in mortified discomfiture, studying the carpet, 'but I just wanted to...I just wanted to do something you would like for a change—'

'Something I would like,' Damiano repeated in a roughened undertone that sent a current of alarm down her spine. 'Like a sort of *big* reward for me coming home alive—'

Eden paled. 'It wasn't like that—'

'You had to jump off the teetotal wagon to do it too,' Damiano continued grittily as if she hadn't spoken. 'A sexual invitation in broad daylight, no less—'

The tension in the atmosphere gave her a panicky sensation in her tummy and once again she tried to intercede. 'Damiano—'

'I think I need to make one thing clear *before* we go to Italy,' Damiano murmured with a chilling bite that took her back five long years. 'I don't want you doing anything solely to please me.'

'Sorry...?'

Damiano studied her bewildered face with grim intensity. 'Do you think I want you pandering to me like some harem slave trying to gratify her owner?' he demanded with icy distaste. 'Do you really think I'm that desperate?'

'I was just trying to show you how much you meant to me,' Eden framed with desperate dignity, hurriedly turning away from him before she broke down. Like some harem slave? She cringed at that label.

His long, lean, powerful body tensing in receipt of that patently sincere response, Damiano expelled his breath in an abrupt hiss. 'I'm sorry—'

'No, I'm sorry that I'm *still* such a big let-down—'

From behind her, Damiano closed his arms around her but Eden was rigid with the pain she was holding in. 'That's not true, *cara*—'

'Yes, it is...you didn't want me,' she pointed out chokily.

'*Per amor di Dio!* Is that what you think?' Damiano groaned above her head, his strong arms wound round her tightly. 'What do you think kept me going in that bloody hell-hole of a prison? Inspiring recollections of making deals at the bank?' His dark, deep drawl dismissed that idea with incredulous scorn. 'It was the thought of you...and the prayer that you would still be waiting for me when I got out of there!'

In astonishment, Eden stiffened, afraid to believe and then desperately wanting to believe what he was telling her. Tears of joy and relief shone in her eyes. 'Then wh-why—?'

'Am I ranting and raving at you?' Damiano filled in jaggedly and, unusually, he hesitated before continuing. 'I think possibly lack of sleep and feeling very claustrophobic in these surroundings.'

Claustrophobic? Eden was suddenly aghast at her own stupidity. When he had mentioned needing space around him, she had totally misunderstood. It was indeed a *very* small flat, the sitting room the only area where two people could move without one continually standing back to let the other pass. And why on earth had she woken Damiano up when he was so exhausted? What strange madness had possessed her?

'You go back to bed,' she urged protectively and she tugged free of his arms with regretful determination. 'If we're being picked up at seven, I have a lot of things to take care of—'

'*Sì*...' Damiano sank down on the bed with lithe grace. 'I suppose you'll need to inform the school that you're resigning—'

'The school?'

'Wherever you're teaching now.' Long lashes lowered over his eyes as he settled back against the pillows and slowly stretched. Still clad in his jeans, he was a devastatingly attractive vision of relaxed masculinity. So powerful was her own response to that awareness that she looked away from him in embarrassment. 'I'm sure you don't like leaving your pupils in the lurch but my need for you is greater, *cara*.'

She supposed it was natural that he should have assumed that she was teaching somewhere. But explaining that the shop below was in fact hers did not seem important just then when further dialogue would mean keeping him awake.

Before she had even finished dressing, Damiano was sound asleep again. She didn't want to leave him. Her heart was behaving as if it had wings attached. She just wanted to sit down at the foot of the bed and revel in the reality that he was physically there. Damiano had said he *needed* her. Damiano had confessed that it had been the memory of her and the thought of coming home to her which had sustained him through his ordeal in Montavia.

However, she had arrangements to make. Refusing to dwell on the intimidating prospect of returning to the Braganzi town house even for just a couple of nights, she packed a case. Fortunately her assistant, Pam Jenkinson, lived nearby and Eden was grateful to find the older woman at home when she called. The year before, Pam had looked after the shop for several weeks when Eden's father had been dying. A prosperous widow, Pam had enjoyed being left in charge and indeed had already stated her interest in taking over the business should Eden ever wish to sell up. However, now, the older woman also wanted every tiny detail ironed out and it was some time before Eden was able to leave her.

As Eden hurried back to her flat, her restive mind began taking her back into the past again, back to her earliest days with Damiano, and she could not help thinking how ironic it was that *neither* of their families had wanted them to be together...

Damiano's first kiss had frankly frightened the hell out of Eden. That sense of being out of control had spooked her. It had been like sin coming knocking on her door with a thunderous crash. So she'd told herself she wouldn't see him again. Then he'd turned up the next morning and her resistance had crumbled. Right from the start, no matter how hard she'd tried, she'd been unable to fight that powerful desperate need to be with him.

That same weekend, her father had met Damiano. The name Braganzi had meant nothing to the older man but Damiano hadn't been gone five minutes before her parent had voiced his dour disapproval. 'Not our sort, is he? And you're not his. He's one of the bosses, Eden—'

'I work for the education authority, not the Falcarragh estate—'

'Folk will talk if you start running about with him and I don't want to hear loose talk about my daughter,' her father asserted grimly.

Eden had to reach the age of twenty-one before she could rebel against a stern paternal dictum. Over Damiano, she rebelled but only within certain boundaries.

'What do you mean you have to be home by midnight?' Damiano enquired with considerable amusement at their next meeting. 'Even Cinderella only lost a shoe. Does your father think you're only at risk of seduction *after* midnight strikes?'

'Please don't make fun of my father—'

Damiano meshed long fingers into her silky hair to make her raise her head again, a rueful smile chasing the mockery from his darkly handsome features. 'You're so ridiculously old-fashioned—'

'By *your* standards, not my own.'

'Pious too,' he muttered, caressing her lips with his own, making her shiver and then tense. 'I've been patient for three days. You *want* me.'

Yes and no, she might have told him had she had the courage. The more she felt that overwhelming excitement threatening, the harder she fought it to stay in control. Already she was beginning to instinctively pull back and freeze him out when he reached for her again. Somehow she set a pattern that she couldn't free herself from even after they married.

The next time Damiano came up to Scotland, he rented a luxury hunting lodge in the hills behind the estate and invited her there for a dinner provided by a chef from a fancy restaurant. At the end of that wonderful meal, Damiano murmured with slumbrous cool, 'Are you staying the night?'

'No.'

Lounging back in his carved dining chair, Damiano fixed sardonic dark golden eyes on her hot face. 'So out of academic interest and the reality that I focus best on a time frame…how many times do I have to see you for you to stay the night?'

'For goodness' sake, there isn't some *stupid* time frame!'

'Then it's the bridal band of gold or nothing,' Damiano countered drily. 'Nothing very spontaneous about that, nothing generous either. In fact, one cannot avoid the obvious conclusion that you're putting a price on your body just like a hooker.'

Pale with rage, Eden rose abruptly from her seat. 'That's it…don't you ever *dare* come near me again!'

'I'm not apologising. I just want a reason that I can understand and I want a warm, giving adult woman—'

'Yes, I imagine you've been with plenty of that sort!' Eden declared in unhidden disgust. 'And where are they now? Do you even remember their names?'

'I can promise you that I'm going to remember you.' Damiano sighed.

'Don't phone me again!' Eden snapped, stalking to the door.

'I wouldn't dream of doing so,' Damiano purred like a jungle cat flexing his claws. 'But you're going to miss me…'

He drove her home without trying to change her mind. She walked in, told her father, 'It's over' and went to bed. That *soon*, she missed him but she would have stood torture rather than admit it. Over the following two weeks, she lost weight, tormented herself with visions of Damiano finding solace with a more sexually available woman and told herself a thousand times that that had really been all he'd been interested in.

At the end of the second week, Damiano landed a helicopter in the field below her home. She was feeding the dogs outside and watched in astonishment as he emerged from the bright yellow chopper. Like a schoolgirl, she climbed the fence and ran to greet him.

'Have you got that reason I can understand worked out for me yet?'

Colouring, she studied the rough grass at his feet and the long dragging silence stretched while he waited. 'I want getting married to feel really special,' she finally admitted jerkily.

'The whole fairy tale. I'm not trying to mock your aspirations but I hear that first-time experiences aren't always that great—'

'That doesn't matter—'

'You missed me?'

'Yes—'

'How much?'

'Too much,' she whispered shakily.

'Good...come fly with me the only place you'll let me fly you, *cara*,' Damiano drawled wryly, closing a possessive arm round her and urging her back towards the helicopter. From that moment on, he respected her boundaries.

He returned to London that same night. Home from agricultural college, Mark Anstey called in the next day. 'Dad tells me you're dating Damiano Braganzi...*wow*!'

And from Mark, she heard all that she should have heard first from Damiano. About the bank, the estate, the fabulous wealth, the top-drawer blue-blooded pedigree.

'Why didn't your father say anything?' she mumbled in shock. 'Even to my father?'

'Braganzi expressed a desire for what he termed "privacy". And as my father said, if a billionaire wants privacy and you like your job, you keep your mouth shut.'

'Why didn't you tell me?' Eden asked Damiano in bewilderment that night on the phone.

'I didn't *not* tell you anything. You simply didn't ask the right questions.'

And he had told no lies either but she had definitely picked up the feeling that Damiano would have preferred her to remain in the dark until he himself chose to disclose his true status in life.

'What are you doing with someone like me?' she muttered, although she tried hard not to ask that question.

'The guy who has everything needs a challenge? Do you think your father might now do something other than grunt antisocially in my direction?'

'No, he's more likely to lock the door and pretend we're out the next time you come calling!' Eden groaned.

But only one short month later, Damiano suggested that they get married. 'I haven't got the time to keep on flying up here—'

'You hardly know me—'

'You want me to do seven years and then another seven years like Jacob in the bible?'

'Marriage is a big step—'

'*Sì, tesoro mio*...but we get to share a bed, don't we?'

And she got nowhere when she tried to pin him down to saying anything more serious.

'It'll not work,' her father forecast dourly to Damiano's face. 'You'll both be sorry. Eden's got no more idea of your life than you have of ours. She won't fit and she'll be miserable.'

'Nothing like being greeted with open arms by the in-law-to-be,' Damiano quipped out of her parent's hearing in the aftermath of the longest, bluntest speech Eden had ever heard the older man make.

Damiano then applied for a special licence and persuaded her into agreeing to a quiet ceremony the very next week. In her heart, she had known it was all too quick and that he was too casual altogether in his attitude. He told her how much he *wanted* her but he never mentioned love. But loving him as she did, she suppressed her every misgiving. He was marrying her. It was her ultimate dream.

She did not meet Damiano's family until they came north for the wedding.

'You do realise that my brother is still in love with Annabel?' Cosetta remarked casually at the small reception which followed at the hunting lodge.

'Who's Annabel?' Eden whispered, never having heard that name before.

'A lady who wouldn't be seen dead in that home-made wedding shroud you're wearing! But then Annabel is one of *us*,' Cosetta asserted cuttingly. 'Privately educated and from a decent social background. Damiano hasn't even mentioned her, has he? What does that tell you?'

'That she wasn't as important to him as you seem to think,' Eden dared to suggest.

'The woman he was engaged to for two years? Think

again. He's on the rebound. They only broke up three months ago. He was crazy about her and then they had some stupid argument. Damiano's far too macho to admit himself at fault. He'll live to regret that when he starts comparing the two of you.'

The flight to their honeymoon in Sicily started with an argument, Eden making tearful accusations on the score of her not having been told about Annabel, Damiano telling her that getting married didn't mean she had the right to interrogate him about his past. Then she began feeling unwell.

'Wedding-night nerves add to the pressure,' Damiano informed her. 'I did warn you that the fairy tale might be hard to capture in reality.'

She fainted when they landed in Sicily. A doctor came out to their fabulous villa and diagnosed the flu.

'In sickness and in health…you do love to throw me in the deep end, *cara.*' Damiano teased, trying to calm her down and comfort her while she sobbed out repeated apologies and felt like a total bridal let-down.

It was well over a week before they finally shared the same bed and consummated their marriage. And that long-awaited experience *was*…disastrous! Damiano then rode roughshod over her every mortified, indeed hysterical protest and insisted on getting the doctor out again to examine her to ensure that she was essentially undamaged by his attentions.

'You've just been one of the unlucky ones,' the medical man said.

The barrier of her virginity had been more than usually resistant. Making love for the first time had hurt much more than she had expected. In the circumstances that had been unavoidable but Damiano had still shouldered guilt for having caused her pain. Eden had been utterly wretched after what she had considered absolute humiliation.

'I suppose I'm really, really lucky that I *didn't* make it into bed with you before we got to the altar, *cara*,' Damiano commented on a reflective footnote. 'You would never have agreed to see me again in this lifetime.'

And looking back from the vantage point of five years of greater maturity, Eden returned to the present with a stifled groan over her own behaviour. She had come back from their honeymoon full of self-pity and hurt pride. She had *leapt* at the idea of separate bedrooms.

Throwing off that memory, knowing that she was a lot wiser than she had once been, Eden hurried back upstairs to her flat. In the hall, she froze at the sight of the rumpled but empty bed she could see through the bedroom door. Then she heard Damiano talking in husky Italian in the sitting room and she just sagged, skin turning clammy with relief. The truth was that, right now, she really could not *bear* Damiano out of her sight. Leaving him even briefly had entailed overcoming the ridiculously childish terror that if she left him alone, he might vanish again!

As she appeared in the doorway Damiano tossed aside his mobile phone. His black hair still damp from the shower, he was fully dressed again but not in the casual jeans he had worn earlier. A superb charcoal-grey suit, worn with a white shirt and silk tie, now sheathed his tall, well-built frame. Smooth expensive cloth outlined his wide shoulders and long powerful thighs with the exquisite perfection of fit only obtainable from a master tailor.

For a split second, it was as if time had swept her

back five years. He was the very image of a rich and powerful banker again. He looked fantastic but at the same time as he stirred her senses he also intimidated her. 'I thought you would still be in bed,' she began uneasily. 'Where did you get that suit?'

'It was delivered to me at Heathrow. Nuncio had my measurements faxed to my tailor before we even left Brazil,' Damiano drawled, a wry curve to his expressive mouth. 'I think he thought shares might crash if I made a public appearance in denim. I've also moved up our departure from here by half an hour. Where have you been?'

She told him about her garment alterations business on the ground floor. Damiano listened in silence, stunning dark eyes flaring with sudden exasperation. 'You've been *sewing* to make a living? What necessity was there for you to sink to that level?'

Colour flew into Eden's cheeks. 'I—'

'I spoke to Nuncio while you were out,' Damiano informed her drily. 'I believe he repeatedly attempted to set up a financial support package for you before you left our home but you refused it.'

In the tense silence, the phone began ringing.

Eden ignored it, dismayed that Damiano was already making judgements about events which had taken place during his absence. 'Damiano—'

'Answer the phone,' Damiano interrupted with stark impatience. 'It's been ringing every ten minutes since you went out!'

No darned wonder he had got back out of bed and given up on getting any further rest! And, of course, he would not have answered her phone when he would not have wished to identify himself and risk having his whereabouts confirmed, thereby inviting the descent of the press on her doorstep. Her conscience twanging as if *she* had been that incessant caller, she answered the phone.

'Eden?'

It was Mark Anstey's voice. As it had been a couple of months since she had heard from him, she was a little surprised but she smiled. 'Mark?'

'Glad I've finally got hold of you!' Mark said urgently. 'I caught a news bulletin on the radio at lunchtime. Tell me, is there any truth in the wild rumour that your long-lost husband has turned up alive and kicking and is now back in England?'

Eden tensed at the apparent fact that word of Damiano's return had already moved into the public domain. 'Yes...yes, there is—'

'Incredible! Is Damiano there with you right now?'

'Yes—'

'Can he hear what you're saying?' Mark continued in a conspiratorial tone.

Discomfited by that question, Eden reddened. 'Well, yes but *why*—?'

'Have you got around yet to mentioning those dirty weekends we're supposed to have enjoyed together?'

Eden froze in dismay at that brutally blunt question and lost colour. 'No...'

'*Don't* mention that tabloid story! Take my advice and keep it quiet for now. Tina will *never* tell the truth,' Mark asserted with even stronger emphasis. 'In fact, I think we need to meet up to discuss this situation face to face as soon as possible—'

At that moment the very last thing Eden wanted to think about was the unpleasant consequences of Mark's affair with Nuncio's wife, Tina, four years earlier. 'I'm sorry but I really couldn't manage that right now—'

'Eden…this *isn't* something you can run away from.'
Something in Mark's voice roused the oddest sense of
foreboding inside Eden.

'Look, I'll be in touch with you very soon!' Eden
swore in a rush and she replaced the receiver in equal
haste before Mark could say anything else to upset her.

She turned back to Damiano, rigid with discomfiture.
Mark had just urged her to keep a secret from her husband. Her conscience could have done without that reminder of what she was already doing! But being so
short with Mark also left her feeling disloyal and un-
grateful for, in the aftermath of his disastrous affair with
Tina, Mark had promised that should the occasion ever
arise he would tell Damiano the truth and clear Eden's
name.

Damiano was very still, his strong bone-structure
fiercely taut. Scorching golden eyes connected with her
evasive gaze and held her fast before she could look
away again.

'So Mark, the love of your life, is still hanging around
five years on,' Damiano breathed chillingly. 'What are
you trying to hide from me?'

In the electric silence of her appalled paralysis, the
doorbell buzzed.

CHAPTER FOUR

THE chauffeur carted Eden's case down the steep stairs and out to the limousine.

What are you trying to hide from me? Deeply unsettled by Damiano's shrewd recognition of her unease during that phone call from Mark, Eden slid into the limousine. However, just as quickly, she reminded herself that she was innocent of being anything other than her sister-in-law Tina's dupe and she lifted her head high again.

Chagrined colour warmed her complexion for she was affronted by Damiano's derisive reference to Mark as 'the love of your life'. Ironically, Damiano had merely employed the same phrase *she* had once used in rueful self-mockery before they'd married! Since then, she had read magazine articles which urged women to keep a still tongue when men asked nosy questions about previous attachments. How *right* those articles were!

Damiano did not like Mark. That was still fresh news to Eden and she marvelled that she had not previously managed to work that out for herself. But then Damiano might well have liked Mark better had she not confided that, as a teenager, she had been infatuated with the younger man. Recalling that trusting confession of her own youthful immaturity now made her cringe. After all, more than five years earlier, Damiano had been anything but confiding on the infinitely more important subject of *why* he had broken off his engagement to Annabel Stavely!

'I asked you a question,' Damiano reminded her with icy cool. 'Why did you look as guilty as hell while you were speaking to Mark?'

'Probably embarrassment!' Eden threw her head back, golden hair rippling back over her shoulders, green eyes sparkling with sudden annoyance. 'So you can stop acting like some Victorian domestic tyrant questioning his flighty child-wife!'

Taken aback by that angry assurance, Damiano's lean dark features froze. 'I beg your pardon?'

'Mark is my friend and I don't feel that I should have to justify that.' Eden tilted her chin in defiance. 'After all, he was never an *intimate* friend...not like you and Annabel, who as an ex-fiancée was put under my nose practically every day of our marriage!'

'What an exaggeration!' Damiano's wide sensual mouth twisted. 'Annabel was my sister's closest friend. Did you expect me to tell Cosetta that Annabel was no longer welcome in our home?'

'No, indeed. Such a sensitive request would never have occurred to you on *my* account!' Eden slammed back at him helplessly as the humiliation of a hundred whispered giggling conversations and scornful glances surfaced in her memory like rocks on which she might still run aground. Annabel and Cosetta had worked together to undermine Eden's every attempt to feel secure in her position as Damiano's wife.

'*Accidenti—*'

'You made me put up with Annabel,' Eden recalled bitterly. 'I wasn't allowed to be possessive...in fact, you called me silly and petty and spiteful when I suggested that your sister could socialise with Annabel some place other than our home, so you can just put up with my fondness for Mark's company!'

'Is that a fact?' Damiano drawled smoothly.

'Yes, that is a fact.' Clashing unwarily with eyes as broodingly dark as a stormy night, Eden then found herself subsiding like a pricked balloon. Indeed, a sense of panic once again gripped her for she was frightened by the undeniable urge she seemed to have to hurl recriminations about the past. Right now their relationship was too fragile to bear the strain.

'I knew you felt threatened by Annabel back then,' Damiano asserted, taking her very much aback with that admission. 'I liked the idea that you were jealous. In those days, I liked punishments of that variety. It was my version of the whip and the chair.'

Focusing on him with truly shocked intensity, Eden parted her lips and then slowly closed them again.

'Manipulative wheels within wheels, a war of attrition which you were in no way equipped to fight, *cara*,' Damiano conceded with wry regret, reaching out to close his hand over her tensely curled fingers where they rested on the seat. 'You really didn't have a clue what was going on beneath the surface of our marriage, did you?'

'No,' she conceded unevenly, colliding with his stunning dark eyes, rational thought suspended, for in the back of her mind she knew that if she actually thought through what he had just smoothly admitted, it would scare the life out of her to accept that he had once played such dangerous and hurtful games with her.

'Never again,' Damiano swore softly, unfurling her taut fingers within his and drawing her closer.

Her heartbeat speeded up. Suddenly she was very short of breath. Gazing into those spectacular eyes smouldering with golden highlights, she felt a little burst of heat ignite deep within her and her colour heightened. He was taking his time but she was just desperate for him to touch her, so desperate that she trembled with anticipation.

'Nothing has to be rushed,' Damiano murmured with slumbrous cool.

Her free hand clenched into his shoulder to steady herself. She could not have agreed with him. Even that dark, deep, sexy drawl of his did something extraordinary to her senses and, brought that close to his lithe, powerful frame, it was as if her body were being whirled into the eye of the storm and out of her control. The straining peaks of her breasts tingled and tightened within her clothing. Lacing his fingers into her silky hair, Damiano let the tip of his tongue delve in a provocative flicker between her soft lips. She jerked as if he had burnt her, a flood of such hunger released, she closed her eyes in quivering aftershock.

'I'm not about to fall on you like a sex-starved animal,' Damiano asserted a shade raggedly, his husky sexy vowel sounds running together. 'Try to relax.'

Not while she was the victim of her own most secret memories. Her mind filled with erotic recollections of Damiano pinning her to the bed with dominant male sexual power and driving her out of her mind with pleasure, she felt utterly wanton.

'Try to stop shaking,.' Damiano urged, sounding more than a little pained. 'I promise not to do anything you don't want to do—'

Eden tore her other hand free of his hold and curved it to the back of his well-shaped head in near desperation. 'Kiss me...*please*.'

Long fingers cupped her cheekbone. 'Eden—?'

'Shut up!' she gasped and pushed her mouth in a blind seeking gesture against his.

For a split second, Damiano was absolutely motionless. Then he tugged her head back to make access easier and crushed her eager mouth to his with a raw, deep urgency that her body recognised with surging joyous response. White-hot excitement engulfed her in a scorching wave. A formless little sound broke low in her throat as sensual reaction slivered through her every skin cell, leaving her weak as water but as attached to Damiano's hard, muscular physique as a vine.

However, he set her back from him. Eden opened passion-glazed eyes and attempted to breathe again. She was maddeningly conscious of the dampness between her thighs and of the extraordinary ache of craving he could awake in her so easily, but she was trying not to be ashamed of that reality in the way she had once been.

Damiano surveyed her from beneath semi-lowered long ebony lashes, feverish colour lying along his taut cheekbones in a scoring line. The thick silence smouldered. 'We're at the airfield,' he stated not quite evenly, scanning her hot face and the sudden downward dip of her eyes.

Wasn't a little enthusiasm what he had always wanted from her? Did he find it unfeminine? Or was he pleased? Unable to bring herself to look at him in case she discovered that once again she had done the wrong thing, Eden said nothing. Still all of a quiver, she climbed out of the limo on wobbly legs. What sort of a welcome would she receive from the rest of the Braganzi family? Her tummy lurched at the prospect. For Eden, it would be a very distasteful meeting.

When they landed at Heathrow, bodyguards met Eden and Damiano, ready to protect them from harassment should the paparazzi appear. Eden was relieved when they were able to leave the airport without incident. But tomorrow a press announcement would be made. Damiano's return from the dead was a major news scoop. The paparazzi would be desperate to track Damiano down to gain that all-important first picture of him.

Inside the unremarkable saloon car, chosen in place of a more noticeable limousine, Eden's hands trembled as she nervously smoothed down her dress. As the press turned the media spotlights back on to Damiano, would one of the newspapers choose to resurrect the allegations made against her three months after her husband had gone missing? Her blood ran cold inside her veins. That photograph which had been printed had looked so utterly damning. While the face of the woman in Mark's arms had been concealed, the registration of the car beside which they had stood had been distinct and that car had, at that time, been Eden's.

The sheer emotional surge of a most extraordinary day was now catching up on Eden fast and she felt incredibly tired. They entered the town house from the mews garages at the rear. Struggling just to keep her eyes open, Eden was past caring about the reception she was likely to receive.

In the grand hall, Damiano paused to rest dark, deep-set eyes levelly on her. 'I'm not expecting you to mend fences with my family tonight. Everybody is under too much strain at present.'

But even that concessionary assurance filled Eden with dismay for, without realising that he was asking for a virtual miracle, Damiano was warning her that he *did* expect her to heal those divisions some time soon. Before she could comment, however, her attention was distracted by the sight of a large photograph of Annabel Stavely prominently displayed on a side table. The undeniably gorgeous redhead, who had once had the power to drive Eden mad with jealousy, had one arm curved round a cute little boy with dark hair, presumably her son.

As Damiano thrust open the drawing-room door and stood back for Eden to precede him, Eden was assuring herself that she couldn't care less about the Braganzi clan's partiality for an ex-fiancée who should have been ancient history. Her eyes cloaked, Eden then scanned the three occupants of the elegant room with its coldly impressive blue decor. Nuncio was already moving towards them. Although he was four years younger than Damiano, he actually looked older. Stocky and portly, he had a weak jawline and brown spaniel eyes.

'Back home where you belong, Damiano!' Nuncio exclaimed in an emotional burst, coming between them to grasp Damiano by the arms and hug him again.

Damiano had probably been hugged all the way back from Brazil. Eden reckoned that Nuncio's slavish attachment to his elder brother was probably the only thing that she could now like about him. Cosetta, Damiano's sister, eight years his junior, remained by the fireplace, her dark eyes challenging Eden with derisive distaste.

Tina, Nuncio's wife, approached with an uncertain smile, like someone shyly testing the water but eager to please. But then Tina had always kept well in with Damiano, Eden recalled painfully, and, over five years back, getting friendly with Damiano's naive wife had just been part of that same self-serving strategy.

The Italian woman was small and blonde just like Eden but there the resemblance ended. Tina had had an oval face with delft-blue eyes and a Cupid's bow mouth. 'How are you, Eden?'

'Eden's exhausted by all the excitement and I'm sure you'll excuse her,' Damiano intervened to answer for his wife. 'Why don't you take her upstairs, Tina?'

Eden left the room in Tina's company, grudgingly amused by what Damiano no doubt saw as a smooth move. Knowing that she had once been close to Tina, he probably thought he was doing her a favour in giving them the privacy to talk.

'Well…you being here with Damiano is quite a surprise, isn't it?' Tina remarked.

That almost childlike little voice sent an absolute shiver down Eden's spine. But then Nuncio's wife had perfected her non-threatening camouflage long before Eden had entered the family. Nuncio had been a student when he'd met Tina, who was seven years older. Tina had fallen pregnant at supersonic speed and had persuaded Nuncio into a quick marriage behind his big brother's back.

Ignoring the other woman's leading comment, Eden said proposally, 'How is my niece, Allegra, doing?'

Tina frowned at that reference to her six-year-old daughter and could not hide her irritation. 'Fine. She's in a boarding-school now.'

It was little comfort that she could now see so clearly through the other woman, Eden conceded. Over five years back, as an insecure new bride, Eden had been eager to believe that she had found a close friend in Tina and shocked to realise too late that she had fallen for the act of a woman who would do whatever it took to protect herself, regardless of how low she had to sink.

Reaching the imposing landing, Eden turned towards the bedroom that had always been hers.

'I'm sorry but Annabel and little Peter use those rooms when they're staying now.' Tina's apologetic intervention was saccharine-sweet. 'I'm afraid I just haven't had time to rearrange things yet.'

Staggered by that explanation, Eden suppressed a surge of pure raging disbelief. Annabel Stavely and her son had been allowed to take over the principal bedrooms in the house when they came visiting? What kind of a nonsensical arrangement was that?

Tina showed Eden into a guest room some distance down a corridor.

'You haven't forgiven me yet, have you?' Tina sighed.

Eden tensed. 'I don't think we should talk about the past—'

'But you can't ignore what's going on right now. Nuncio is just *dying* to tell Damiano about Mark and he won't keep quiet on your behalf for ever!'

'On *my* behalf?' Eden queried gently. 'You're the one who had the affair, Tina.'

'No comment.' Open ridicule gleamed in Tina's bright blue eyes.

'Five years ago, the tabloid press assumed that the woman in that photograph with Mark was me. I covered for you,' Eden reminded the other woman, provoked by her mockery. 'I didn't *want* to do it! But you persuaded me that it would be horribly selfish to tell the truth and cause trouble between you and Nuncio—'

'Well, so it would have been! After all, I was a mother as well as a wife. I had Allegra to consider and I didn't think that Damiano would *ever* be coming back!' Tina cut in defensively. 'Naturally I was grateful for what you did for me—'

'So *grateful* that as soon as you felt safe from exposure you joined Nuncio and Cosetta in calling me a slut and attacking me at every turn!' Eden interrupted with pained recollection of what she had had to endure. 'I was forced out of this house and you were just as keen as the others to see me gone!'

'Can't you understand that I was afraid that Nuncio might start suspecting *me* if I didn't play along?'

'All I understand is that while I was grieving for my husband, I took a heavy punishment for something I didn't do,' Eden framed ruefully. 'And you have to accept that if talk of that affair should surface again, I'll be telling Damiano the truth—'

'And I'll say you're lying! Who's going to believe your version this long after the event? Don't forget how much *you* were seen to lean on Mark after Damiano went missing.' Tina stressed with scorn. 'That's all anybody will remember.'

Eden paled. She saw what a fool she had been to allow herself to be bullied into protecting the other woman almost five years earlier. Tina had talked of her shame, her regret and of how much she had still loved Nuncio. Eden had been made to feel so guilty about her desire to defend her own reputation. Tina had been her friend. And all Eden had had to do was allow the assumption that *she* was the woman in that photograph to stand unchallenged. Unfortunately the consequences of shielding Tina had been far greater than Eden had foolishly foreseen.

'I honestly don't believe that Damiano would go tattling to Nuncio…oh, for goodness' sake, Tina,' Eden muttered in weary and distressed appeal. 'I told you that if Damiano ever came home to me, he would have to be told the real story and you agreed—'

'Of course I did.' Tina gave her a catlike smile of

acknowledgement on that point. 'I married a useless lump of lard but he's a very rich lump and there is *nothing* that I wouldn't do to fight my own corner!'

Eden studied the older woman with shaken recoil from that description of Nuncio.

Tina dealt her an even more disconcerting look of malicious amusement. 'Nobody will ever believe that I was the unfaithful wife, so you're in no position to threaten me—'

'I'm *not* threatening you—'

'You've got one *huge* shock coming your way in any case,' Tina murmured with venomous softness. 'But being sworn to secrecy by all parties concerned, I dare not let that particular cat out of the bag. Wait and see whether or not *your* marriage has a future before you waste your time *trying* to wreck mine!'

As the door closed on the blonde's triumphant exit, Eden was genuinely bewildered. 'One huge shock'? What on earth was Tina trying to suggest? Tired as she was, Eden took a quick shower in the *en suite* to freshen up. She only wished she could as easily wash away the memory of Tina's spite. Pure and pointless, spite, that's all it was, she told herself. At least Mark had no personal axe to grind over his affair with Tina, she reflected with relief. Damiano might not particularly like Mark but, if she needed Mark to clear her own name, he would surely accept the younger man's word.

Her suitcase still sat just inside the bedroom door. In spite of the fact that no Braganzi expected or indeed usually received anything less than twenty-four-hour domestic service, nobody had come to unpack for her. Eden smiled at the fact that she was feeling slighted and tugged out a nightdress. Clambering into the big comfortable bed, she wondered how long it would take Damiano to come upstairs and join her.

Eden had actually drifted off to sleep when a loud noise interspersed with raw male invective woke her up with a start. She sat up and switched on the light. Damiano, lean strong face grim with anger, had evidently tripped over her case in the dark.

'Are there no maids in this house? And why have you chosen to sleep so far away from me that I have to go on a major search to find you in my own home?' Damiano demanded with eloquent outrage, striding over to the bed, trailing back the duvet and scooping her off the divan without a second of hesitation.

'What on—?' she gasped.

Heading out into the corridor again with her still gripped in his powerful arms, Damiano breathed flatly, 'We share the same room, the same bed.'

Settled down on to a bed in a much more impressive room situated off the main landing, Eden flushed. 'Sleeping elsewhere wasn't my idea—'

'*Per meraviglia!* Do I look dumb enough to believe that?' Damiano was crushingly unimpressed by her plea of innocence.

Slinging his jacket on a chair, he swept up the internal phone to communicate terse instructions to some member of staff. As he spoke, he unknotted his tie and tossed it aside and began unbuttoning his shirt. Dry-mouthed, heartbeat accelerating, aware of the thunderous tension he was now exuding in primal waves but unable to concentrate on it, Eden watched him as he completed the call.

Languor was spreading through her body like a flood of warm honey. Even furious, he was breathtakingly beautiful to her mesmerised eyes. Her breathing fractured as he let the shirt drop where he stood. Six feet four inches of vibrant bronzed masculinity, wide, smooth shoulders, broad chest, taut, flat stomach, all rippling whipcord muscles.

Without warning, Damiano flashed a glance at her and stilled, aggressive jawline squaring. *'What?'*

Eden jerked. 'Sorry?'

Damiano spread two not quite steady hands wide, dark eyes blazing gold. 'I'm damned if I'm going into the bathroom to undress. Just close your eyes!'

'But, Damiano, I *wasn't.*'

'I've gone nearly forty-eight hours without sleep,' Damiano grated in a savage undertone. 'Just get under the sheet, turn your back and pretend you're on your own!'

Her teeth clenched. She hauled up the sheet and flipped over on to her side. Why was he so set on misunderstanding her? She tautened. He was interpreting her behaviour against a five-year-old yardstick and what else could he do?

'I'm not as prudish as I used to be!'' Eden whispered in a defensive hiss. 'I've grown up a lot!'

The mattress gave, the lights snapped off and Damiano reached for her with both hands, hauling her up against him and shocking her into silence. 'Grown women don't need to fill up on vodka first, *cara,*' he muttered thickly into her hair, dark, deep drawl steadily lowering in pitch and clarity as his big powerful frame relaxed. 'If I had an ego problem, you'd have made me impotent. I spent seven months of marriage listening to every excuse not to have sex that has ever been invented. I spent most of the next five years between a prison cell and a quarry. I'm sure I was the only guy there who fantasised about a wife in a nightdress because he had never ever seen her naked!'

Trembling with mortification, tears stinging her eyes, Eden gulped and swallowed hard.

Damiano released a sleepy sigh. 'But you love me. On your terms, the shoes you wore to bed this afternoon were a massive statement of devotion. Right now, I'll settle for that.'

Right now? She opened her eyes, wildly conscious of his proximity, the sexy masculine scent of him, the heat he emanated. But he was now holding her at a slight distance from him. She swallowed again, wanting him so much she was burning all over. Finally, she moistened her lips and parted them. 'I don't need the vodka...'

Only silence greeted that announcement. She listened to the deep, even tenor of his breathing and rubbed her cheek helplessly against his hand where it rested loosely on the pillow. She had him back. It was enough. Whatever he wanted, he could have...she just wouldn't make her efforts to please so obvious the next time. She loved him *so* much. Even the family from hell wasn't going to part them!

At what felt like the crack of dawn the next morning, Damiano woke her up. Exuding cool self-command, Damiano was already fully dressed in a dark business suit, burgundy silk tie and a pearl-grey silk shirt. His stunning dark eyes rested on her with a slumbrous quality that drove her mind blank and sent her heartbeat racing.

'I have a press conference set up for ten,' Damiano drawled.

'Oh...' Her tummy flipping at the mere thought of attending a press conference, Eden paled.

'It'll be a circus and not your style. There's no need for you to come, *cara*.' Damiano sank fluidly down on the edge of the bed, brilliant eyes shimmering over her. 'I'm spending the afternoon with a whole collection of bankers and lawyers. I think it would be wisest if we fly out to Italy separately—'

'Separately?'

'I'm determined to keep our destination a secret from the paparazzi. One of my bodyguards will accompany you on a private flight this afternoon. I'll meet you at the villa…it could well be tomorrow before I make it.'

A sharp rap sounded on the door.

Exasperation flashing across his darkly handsome features, Damiano vaulted upright and strode over to answer it. Eden recognised Nuncio's anxious voice.

Before he departed, Damiano glanced back at her with a wry smile. 'The villa is, I believe, larger than a rabbit hutch and it is *not* communal,' he assured her with admirable cool.

Just a few more hours and she would be on her way to Italy. A sunny smile curved Eden's lips. A maid arrived with a breakfast tray laden with all Eden's favourite dishes. She had just finished eating when the phone by the bed buzzed.

The caller was Mark.

'How on earth did you work out where I was?' Eden asked in confusion.

'It hardly took genius. I was once a regular visitor to the town house,' Mark reminded her impatiently. 'Look, I've come up to London specially and I'd like to see you as soon as possible.'

And why shouldn't she see Mark before she left for Italy? Eden suddenly asked herself. He was a good friend and, although he had his flaws, she had never forgotten his sympathetic support in the aftermath of Damiano's disappearance. No doubt, Mark would also enjoy hearing the inside story on Damiano's return home. And shouldn't she tell Mark that, exactly as he had forecast, Tina was determined to lie about their affair?

Mark suggested that she meet him at his hotel. Eden called a cab to pick her up and she slipped out of the house by the rear entrance. A slimly built young man with dark blond hair and pale blue eyes, Mark, as elegantly dressed as always, was waiting for her in the lobby.

Eden accompanied him into the almost empty residents' lounge. 'It's so good to see you again,' she said warmly.

'Tell me what's been happening on the home front,' Mark invited, having ordered tea for Eden and a drink for himself.

'I was going to ask you how you've been doing first,' Eden told him ruefully. 'I haven't heard much from you lately.'

'I think your situation is rather more important right now.'

Eden grimaced. 'Well, what you said over four years ago has been borne out. You said I was a real fool to take the heat for Tina and you were right. It *has* come back to haunt me. Tina is still treating me like her worst enemy and Nuncio is eagerly waiting for me to make a full confession to Damiano. The sooner the whole wretched business is cleared up, the better.'

'So you *will* be wanting me to support your story?'

Eden flushed. 'I hope it won't come to that. That would be embarrassing for you—'

'I'll tell Damiano anything you like.' Mark shrugged. '*But*...I'm afraid there'll be a price.'

Her brow furrowed. 'A price?'

'Let me tell you a story.' Mark's mouth took on a sullen twist as he studied her. 'My longest-standing friend marries a fabulously wealthy bloke and what does she do to help me?'

Eden went rigid. 'What are you getting at?'

'You got me a lousy first job working for peanuts on the Braganzi country estate!' Mark derided. 'And when I asked for the cash to set up my own business, you said you were sorry but Damiano thought I was too young to be trusted with that size of an investment.'

Mark was delving way back to events which had occurred in the first months of Eden's marriage. At the time, those events had made Eden feel very uncomfortable with both her husband and Mark. 'I didn't realize you still felt like that about—'

'No, of course you didn't. Damiano went missing soon afterwards and I decided the rich Mrs Braganzi was a long-term investment to be nursed along.' Beneath her stricken gaze, Mark vented a sour laugh. 'Just two more years and Damiano would have been legally presumed dead. No matter how hard his relatives fought, you would still have copped most of the loot as Damiano's wife! Would you have been generous then, Eden? That *was* what I was waiting for—'

'I can't believe you really mean what you're saying...' A queasy sensation of mounting fear was engulfing Eden. 'You were so kind to me after Damiano disappeared.'

'But you'll have to pay me to get service like that again. I won't admit that I had that affair with Tina unless you make it well worth my while…if you don't, I'll take Tina's side and drop you in it with Damiano—'

'That's sick!' Eden gasped and then, realising that she had attracted the attention of the elderly woman seated at the far end of the room, she reddened fiercely.

'Think *very* hard before you tell me to go ahead and do my worst,' Mark advised thinly.

'But to try to blackmail me…' Eden condemned shakily.

Only now was she recalling Mark's bitter resentment when Damiano had refused to invest in him until he had more business experience. She had chosen to forget that unpleasant episode but Mark had just made it brutally clear that he had only continued their friendship beyond that point because he had expected to profit from it. Damiano's survival must have come as a very unwelcome surprise to Mark, she conceded painfully.

'So now I'll tell you what I want…' With complete calm, Mark went on to mention a sum of money that made Eden pale.

'Not all up front at once of course; he conceded grudgingly. 'But I expect a down payment as a guarantee of your good faith. Since you've always been so frank with me, I know exactly what you've got in your bank account. You won't be needing that money for your own use any more so I'll take a cheque now—'

'Mark, *please*—'

'Make your choice. Tina will not hesitate for a second if I approach her with a similar offer,' Mark warned her smugly. 'Then it'll be goodbye to Damiano, Eden.'

Picturing both Tina and Mark conspiring together to destroy her marriage made Eden feel trapped and physically ill. What would her word be worth to Damiano if everybody else swore that she was guilty as hell?

With a trembling hand that seemed to have developed a will of its own, Eden dug into her handbag for her cheque-book. Without looking back at Mark again, she scrawled out the cheque and left it sitting on the table. Then she stood up and walked out of the hotel lounge.

CHAPTER FIVE

IN THE shattered emotional state she was in, Eden wandered round the shops for a while until she got a grip on herself again. She asked herself what sort of a fool she was that she had not seen through Mark to the greed and resentment beneath the surface. She had trusted him absolutely and now he was blackmailing her!

How on earth was she to get out of the dreadful nightmare she had brought down on herself? She was bitterly ashamed of having simply surrendered to Mark's threats. But most of all she now loathed her own blind, trusting stupidity. When the press had exposed that affair and wrongly identified the woman involved, she should not have kept silent to protect Tina. How could she have been that foolish? But she knew how and why. Distraught over losing Damiano, she had been an easy mark for Tina's guile.

As she walked by the electrical section of a big store, Eden's attention was caught by the shock value of seeing Damiano on several television screens at once. The press conference was being televised and a bunch of shoppers was glued to the screens. Having come to a dead halt, Eden moved slowly closer to watch.

The cameras loved Damiano. As he fielded questions with assurance and humour, his natural charisma made him a class act. Every so often a different camera angle would take in the people standing near him. Nuncio, proudly intent on his big brother. A couple of directors of the Braganzi Bank, glowing at Damiano's every witty response, no doubt highly relieved that the male once dubbed a genius in the money markets should have returned with all his faculties intact.

A powerful surge of guilt engulfed Eden then and she turned away. In retrospect, she was ashamed that she had snatched at the excuse Damiano had given her and avoided the press conference. From the moment that tabloid story had been printed nearly five years earlier, she had been terrified of the media. Instead of giving way to that cowardice, she should have fought it and, even though Damiano had not appeared to be in much need of wifely support, she would have been prouder of herself had she at least *offered* it.

Eden was really running quite late by the time she got back to the town house. As she crossed the hall, Tina emerged from the drawing room, looking extremely smug. 'You have about ten minutes to freshen up before you leave for your second honeymoon in Italy.'

Ignoring the blond's honeyed scorn, Eden asked, 'Is Damiano back yet?'

'No, but he did try to call you. He wasn't very pleased when I told him that I hadn't a clue where you were.' A malicious smile curved the older woman's voluptuous mouth. 'Then I took the trouble to call him back and mention that just before you went out, dear old Mark had phoned, given his name and asked to speak to you. Mark was never discreet, was he?'

Paling at Tina's venom but determined not to respond in kind, Eden raced upstairs to change. Over an hour later, she entered the airport, accompanied by a single bodyguard. She was totally unprepared for what happened next. A man with a camera appeared about ten feet away and blinded her by taking a flash photo.

Within the space of sixty seconds, she was the centre of a heaving crowd of reporters shouting questions.

'Why weren't you with your husband at the press conference?'

'Is your marriage in trouble, Mrs Braganzi?'

'Why did the Braganzi family fly out to Brazil without you?'

'Why have you been in hiding all these years?'

If the airport security men hadn't come to their rescue, they would never have managed to escape. White and trembling, Eden only began breathing evenly again when the small private plane took off for Italy. Somebody must have tipped the press off that she would be arriving at the airport. Who? Tina? Or was she so strung up now that she was imagining things?

Whatever, her every worst fear seemed to be coming true. Damiano was big news and, by the same definition, so was the state of his marriage. Her absence from the press conference had evidently created comment. How *long* did she have before that old scandal about her was dug up again?

Late that afternoon, the car which had whisked Eden out of Pisa turned off a twisting mountain road into an avenue hedged and shadowed by tall cypresses. Through a break in the trees, Eden saw a lake with a surface like a silver mirror and then she caught her first glimpse of the Villa Pavone.

The magnificent building was sited on the hilltop. Ornate stucco decorations and a grand run of Ionic columns embellished the villa's impressive frontage. As she got out of the car, the glorious warmth of early summer enfolded her. Citrus trees in giant metal urns dispelled an aromatic scent which hung heavy in the still air. As she moved towards the entrance, an eerie plaintive shriek made her glance nervously over her shoulder. She was just in time to see a glimmer of ghostly white disappear behind a topiary tree. An instant later, a glorious white peacock strutted into view, his fantastic plumage spread like filigree lace. The bird regarded her with expectant beady eyes, seemingly awaiting a burst of appreciative applause.

Eden grinned, the last of her anxiety falling away. She strolled towards the huge front doors which stood wide. The paparazzi were behind her in London along with Damiano's dreadful relatives *and* Mark, she reminded herself cheerfully. In a few hours surely at most, Damiano would be with her again.

She walked into a breathtaking foyer, so big it echoed loudly with her footsteps. The walls were adorned with fabulous classical frescos. Far above her hung a superb gilded and painted ceiling.

'Where the hell were you this morning?'

Eden almost jumped right out of her skin. She spun round, green eyes very wide and startled. Damiano had magically appeared in a doorway which she had not previously noted in her awed scrutiny of her surroundings. 'You're here already?' she gasped in delighted surprise.

He looked incredibly attractive in well-cut beige chinos and a short-sleeved cream cotton shirt that accentuated his bronzed skin and black hair. But Damiano was surveying her with glittering dark eyes, his lean, strong face hard as granite, megawatt tension emanating from the stillness of his long, lithe, powerful frame.

'You were with Mark—'

Eden blinked, tautening. 'Yes,' she conceded jerkily, determined to stick as close to the truth as was possible.

'For *hours*?' Damiano derided harshly. 'You almost missed your flight!'

'No, I didn't cut it that fine,' she countered tightly and curled her tense fingers into her damp palms, the happy sensation draining away, leaving only stress in its wake. 'And I wasn't with him *all* that time. I walked round the shops for a while—'

'You're not telling me the truth.'

The silence started feeling like a giant black hole spreading to within inches of her feet, ready to suck her in at any moment. The confidence with which Damiano made that charge was pure intimidation. It wasn't a question. It wasn't a sneaky carrot designed to draw her into speech and trip her up. No, what she was hearing was the challenge of a very shrewd male, who had not the slightest shred of doubt that she was concealing something from him.

'Why...why do you think that?' Eden prompted drymouthed.

His spectacular golden eyes struck sparks off hers. 'Tell me the truth,' he demanded with ice-cool clarity. 'You're squirming like a fish on a hook.'

Eden worried at her lower lip with her teeth and stared back at him, horribly impressed by his power of perception. 'I...'

'Yes?' Damiano grated in the explosive silence.

'I only trailed round the shops because I was upset and that's why I was so late getting back to the house,' Eden volunteered in a driven rush. 'No big mystery.' She shrugged awkwardly. 'I just saw Mark as I hadn't managed to see him before...and I didn't like what I saw. So for that reason, I *won't* be seeing him again.'

A faint frown-line had appeared between Damiano's winged ebony brows. She registered that she had disconcerted him, had roved wildly off whatever script he had expected her to pursue. 'What—?'

Eden folded her arms in a defensive movement and straightened her slim shoulders. 'Look, it was unpleasant enough finding out that Mark wasn't the wonderful friend I thought he was. I don't need you demanding to hear it all, so that I can feel a right idiot all over again!'

'You've decided to end the friendship?' Damiano seemed to be having a problem grasping that reality. 'When did you decide that? Right there this minute when it dawned on you that I'm angry?'

Her shoulders sagged. 'Oh, boy, are you paranoid...'

Damiano went rigid, faint colour arching across the hard slant of his high cheekbones. 'I merely requested that you explain yourself—'

'And I politely refused to go into any greater detail. Mark's just not important enough for us to be arguing over him.' Eden meant that assurance with every proud fibre of her being.

'*Santa cielo*...I am *not* arguing...where the blazes are you going?' Damiano raked at her in a lion's roar as she began walking back in the direction of the front doors.

'I thought maybe if I went out and then came back in again, you might give me a nicer welcome.'

A dropped feather could have sounded like a thundering avalanche in the rushing silence which followed.

Eden heard Damiano move behind her but she was still quite unprepared to find herself being suddenly snatched right off her feet and up into his powerful arms. For a moment, the world tilted crazily. Then she met the mesmeric lure of his burnished golden eyes. Simultaneously she ran out of breath and rational thought. An instant burst of wanton heat ignited inside her, sending her heartbeat crashing, her pulses pounding.

A scorching smile slashed Damiano's lean, powerful face. 'This is the kind of welcome I should l have given you, *tesoro mio*.'

He pressed his mouth to the tiny pulse flickering like crazy below her delicate collar-bone. Her throat extended, her entire body jerked. She lifted a shaking hand to curve it to his dark head and then his mouth found hers. A huge brilliant fireworks display blazed up in the darkness behind her lowered eyelids. She was so hot, so excited, she clutched wildly at him. He lowered her down onto a hard, cold surface, closed his hands over her knees and parted them so that he could haul her back into even closer contact.

A hoarse little cry of response was wrenched from her as he let his long fingers glide up her slender thighs beneath her dress. She was shivering, shaking, alight with a hunger that burned. Damiano rested his hands on her slim hips and lifted his head to gaze down at her, dark, deep-set eyes shimmering gold, strong face hard with raw male need, beautiful mouth almost ruthless in its line.

'So now you show me that you don't need the vodka,' Damiano murmured in thickened invitation.

For a split second, her veil of desire was pierced by an inner screech of shock. What? *Here? Now? On a marble table?* And then Eden collided with those dark golden eyes that had haunted her dreams from the very hour of their first meeting. She literally felt her body melt. Awareness slid away again. The world could have ended right there and then and she wouldn't have cared.

'I don't mean *here*,' Damiano husked, laughter roughening his rich, deep, sexy drawl.

He tugged her off the table and wound her fingers calmly into his to urge her through the doorway which he had appeared in earlier. Her legs felt weak and wobbly supports. Yet her every skin cell felt almost painfully alive. Sexual tension was twisting her into a deliciously tight knot. Their footsteps echoed as they passed through yet another vast room, full of marble columns, glittering crystal chandeliers and huge oil paintings. As Damiano led her beneath an ornate portal which opened onto the fantastic double flight of stairs which wound gracefully up to the first floor, she was gazing in astonishment at their palatial surroundings.

Upstairs, Damiano walked her into a room that at first glance struck her as the size of an aircraft hangar. A hangar with a bed, that was. And what a bed, overhung by a giant gold coronet from which glorious brocade hangings descended into extravagant folds down onto an exquisite rug. 'You can live the fairy tale like the little princess.'

'You being here with me...' Eden muttered unevenly. 'That's enough of a fairy tale.'

Damiano dealt her a slumbrous sexy look from beneath black spiky lashes. He settled his hands to her slim shoulders and turned her slowly and carefully round. As he ran the zip down on her dress, her breath feathered in her throat. Light was flooding through the tall windows, light so bright she could see dust motes dancing in the air. And she felt terribly shy and self-conscious but she didn't feel like rushing across the room to close the shutters and plunge them into darkness.

Once she had tormented herself with secret humiliating comparisons between Annabel's long-legged voluptuous shape and her own infinitely slighter and smaller attractions. The urge to keep her seeming deficiencies covered from view had risen to obsessive proportions. But in allowing herself to think in that way, she had forgotten the only thing that really mattered. Damiano had married *her*; Damiano had chosen her, *not* Annabel Stavely.

He eased her dress from one slight, taut shoulder, making a production out of the process. She shut her eyes tight. '*Santo Cielo...*' Damiano swore huskily above her head. 'I'm burning for you, *cara*.'

He lifted her hair and bent her head forward and let his expert mouth trail across the exposed nape of her neck. She quivered, every sense leaping. 'Oh...'

'This will be so good,' Damiano promised with husky sensuality.

The very sound of his voice could turn her boneless. A muted little gasp escaped her as her dress drifted down to her ankles. She fought the instinct to cross shielding arms over herself. She could feel the tips of her breasts hardening into straining little points within her bra. She could feel the wave of heat travelling over her and her knees started to wobble.

'You are doing *so* well,' Damiano purred appreciatively. 'You're quivering like a racehorse ready to bolt but you're still in the same room.'

'No vodka,' she mumbled, trying to match him in humour but her voice came out all shaky.

'Open your eyes, *cara*,' Damiano urged as he lifted her clear of the tangle of cloth round her feet and spun her back to him. 'Enjoy me admiring you.'

He was pushing too far too fast. She knew she had small breasts and hips that were just a little too full for the rest of her and legs that were just legs, not especially long or especially anything, sturdy enough to be useful, not flashy enough to attract attention. 'I *can't*!'

'Would you prefer to sleep alone in that bed tonight?'

Her lashes lifted high on stricken green eyes. *'No!'* she gasped with even greater force.

'Gotcha…' Damiano drawled with smouldering satisfaction, brilliant dark golden eyes scanning her blushing face. 'I cheated. You have no chance of sleeping alone.'

Her brow indented. 'No…?'

Bending down, he swept her up again into his arms and strode over to the bed to settle her there. She kicked off her shoes and began scrabbling at the bed linen to get under it.

'Ah…ah…' Damiano allowed her to get under cover and then, hooking long brown fingers round the fine linen sheet, he flipped the bedding deftly back into a fold at the footboard. 'It's a sort of knee-jerk reaction, isn't it? But a little modesty goes a long way with me, *cara.*'

Rather than remain splayed out in only her bra and pants, she sat up again and hugged her knees, hands tightly clasped. She was striving desperately to think of something witty or cool to say. 'I…I, well—'

'Shut up,' Damiano broke in with tender amusement. 'You may not like your body but I *love* it!'

She studied his stunningly attractive features and felt that melting sensation down deep inside that just overwhelmed her. She didn't place much credence in what he said but she knew he wanted her. She had felt the hard urgency of him against her, could not doubt the physical reality of his desire. She watched him peel off his shirt. Her lashes lowered, carefully screening the directness of her gaze, but she was as hopelessly mesmerised by his potent male beauty as she had always been. He had no inhibitions and she adored that blatant, blazing self-assurance he emanated, so very different from her own.

As he unzipped his chinos, exposing the taut, hard flatness of his stomach bisected by a silky dark furrow of hair, a tight little stab of sexual awareness twisted low in her tummy. He was all male, full of dynamic energy and hot-blooded intensity. Shimmying her hips back deeper into the shadows cast by the drapes festooning the bed, Eden watched the chinos being cast aside with keen interest. She studied the long flow of his smooth brown back, the lean masculine hips in pale boxer shorts, the long hair-roughened thighs. She did not look away as she had once done. Indeed she was hot with curiosity to see him totally stripped but terrified that he might notice.

Damiano disposed of the boxer shorts. Her face flamed. Aroused he was distinctly intimidating but it was of the variety of intimidation that filled her with hot, quivery sensations. Suddenly ashamed of what she recognised as pure lust within herself, she dropped her head, no longer able to see anything but Damiano's beautifully shaped brown feet approaching the bed.

The mattress gave slightly under his weight. The silence hummed. She sat there, head lowered over knees.

'You're such a little cheat,' Damiano condemned with a throaty chuckle as he reached for her and tumbled her down against the comfortable pillows.

'Sorry?' Eden spluttered, disconcerted by the swiftness of that move.

Rolling over, Damiano slid a long hard masculine thigh between hers and held her captive beneath his superior weight. He trailed a mocking forefinger along

the curve of her soft lower lip and made it impossible
for her to avoid his intent scrutiny. 'I saw you watching
me.'

He was just inches away. She reddened fiercely. Her
mouth ran dry.

'And...' Damiano dragged out the word '...I also
think you *like* what you saw—'

'No—?'

'*No?*' Damiano questioned, raising a sardonic dark
brow.

'I m-mean yes, but—'

'Don't want to hear the "but".' With a husky growl
of very male gratification, Damiano teased at her mouth
with his own, lighting a trail of fire to run through her
shivering body. Those light, frustrating kisses merely
stoked her growing tension. She squirmed under him
seeking greater force, her own hunger demanding more.

'So tell me you want me,' Damiano invited thickly.

'What?' she framed blankly, fingers curling into his
broad shoulders with a frustration she could not suppress.

'I want to hear the words...' Damiano confided, slid-
ing down the bed and, by so doing, revealing to her for
the first time that he had already somehow contrived to
remove her bra without her noticing.

Dismay flashed through her. *'Damiano!'*

'No, *cara*...' His hands clamped down over her
wrists before she could attempt to cover her bare
breasts. 'You're beautiful...you are really beautiful and
I need to look at you just as much as you like to look
at me,' he spelt out in a devastatingly effective demand
for equal rights.

She trembled, feeling so horrendously vulnerable,
staring down at her pale breasts with their shamelessly

swollen pink nipples. And then she saw Damiano surveying the same view like a hungry tiger, hot golden eyes pinned to her with a visual intensity that shook her. He had already released her wrists but she had little difficulty in resisting her once compulsive need to conceal herself from him. She was now watching him in total fascination. She arched her back slightly, shifted her hips, feeling like a madly seductive stranger beneath such erotic male appreciation.

He was just looking and she was already starting to burn again. He lifted a hand that was noticeably unsteady and curved it to her super-sensitive flesh. He lowered his proud dark head and let the tip of his tongue flick a pouting peak and her whole body just surged up in response. 'I want you!' she moaned, helpless in the grip of that devastating wave of sexual hunger.

Damiano rewarded her with a wolfish smile that made her heart flip over and filled her with such a flood of love that she felt as fluid as water. 'You're all mine,' he breathed raggedly. 'You're the only woman I have ever been with who has only ever been mine. I really get a high out of that.'

He brought his mouth down on hers with an explosive passion that she needed as much as he did. Heartbeat thundering in her eardrums, she gasped as he stroked her breasts and she dug her fingers into the dark silk luxuriance of his hair. She couldn't get enough of that hard, demanding mouth. She strained against him, controlled by the heat and the strength of her own craving, every defence finally abandoned.

'Please…' She gasped, struggling to get breath back into her lungs but desperate to get his hot urgent mouth back on hers again.

'You've changed so much,' Damiano ground out, his

breathing even more fractured than her own as he skimmed an impatient hand down over her quivering length and deftly rearranged her so that he could remove her briefs.

She had never been so conscious of being naked but the daylight had nothing to do with it. Erotic anticipation now fired her. She was reaching for him even before he was reaching for her again. Tiny broken sounds were wrenched from her as he pushed her back against the pillows and employed his lips and his tongue on her tingling breasts with a hard, sensual expertise that was entirely new to her. And, new as that more forceful approach was, it drove her crazy with excitement.

'I never thought I would see you like this...out of your mind with desire for me!' Damiano extended with raw appreciation, black hair tousled, tough cheekbones scored with feverish colour. 'Eden...Eden...'

And even the way he raggedly groaned her name made her react. She was all heat and constant movement. The burning fever that had taken control of her was way beyond anything she had ever experienced. With a sure hand, he found the damp, pulsing heart of her and she cried out loud on the incredible surge of excitement he unleashed.

Glittering golden eyes invaded hers. He was watching her every reaction. Disconcertion tried to penetrate the blinding, all-pervasive sway of passion and for a split second she attempted to regain some measure of control. But she was way beyond that ability and dimly registering that shocked her too, only his dominant control over her was too great by then.

'I...I can't help it...' She tried to say, not really knowing whether she was trying to apologise or not and, if she was, what she might be attempting to say sorry for.

'I *know...*'

She was enslaved, enthralled by the passion, her writhing body entirely ruled by his knowing touch. And in no time at all that oh, so skilled touch became near agonising torment for she wanted...she wanted *so* much. And the hunger was so powerful it was eating her alive and her hands were clinging to him, her hips rising, the ache of emptiness a torment.

'Please...' she begged.

In one lithe movement, Damiano came over her, tipped her back, a devouring need more than equal to her own blazing in his smouldering golden gaze. As he entered her yielding flesh, she uttered a high-pitched moan and jerked in sensual shock from that invasion. Her excitement was at such a pitch by then that she thought she might pass out from the sheer overload of pleasure. The powerful response of her own body gripped her now. Heart crashing, he drove her to the heights she had never known existed. Stunned by the wild ecstatic intensity that shattered her into a million pieces, she sobbed with joyful release and slowly went back into free fall.

Eden's eyes were awash with tears but wide with shock at the same time. Never ever had she imagined she might experience such glorious pleasure.

Damiano released her from his weight and hauled her back into intimate connection with his damp, hot frame. He kissed her breathless and held her back from him, scanning her still shaken face with questioning intensity. 'You truly *didn't* realise that you were missing anything five years ago,' he breathed on the back of a rueful laugh.

'You mean...it's *always* supposed to be like that?' she gasped, too taken aback by the idea to be self-conscious.

'I used to think of spiking your pure orange to make you let go in bed but I knew you would never forgive me.' Damiano splayed long brown fingers round her cheekbones, gazing deep into her incredulous green eyes. 'You just would not relax. You had so many hang-ups. You hit my male ego right where it hurts. The only woman I couldn't satisfy was my wife...'

'I was quite happy with what...well...you know,' she mumbled, thinking in a positive daze at what she had just learned. How could she have known there was more when she had never experienced anything more until now? She remembered pleasure but a pleasure that was frankly mild in comparison with what she had just enjoyed. She remembered liking the start better than the finish and vague feelings of dissatisfaction but nothing she hadn't accepted as normal and natural. From that first painful initiation, she had stubbornly decided that making love would always be something he received more pleasure from than she did.

But there was more to it than that, Eden recognised in sudden shame. She had had resentments of her own from very early in their marriage. The marital home in which she felt like an intruder, the family who had regarded her as a social inferior, Annabel, the ex-fiancée, who wouldn't quit flaunting her own preferential status. She had blamed Damiano for her unhappiness and had made no attempt to overcome her inhibitions. Damiano, she registered with shaken new self-awareness, had not been the *only* one set on a war of attrition...

Damiano curved her to him so that she was plastered to every powerful angle of his indolent length. 'Sex was a taboo subject. You once said that it was bad enough having to do that sort of thing without being expected to talk about it as well,' he groaned.

Eden stifled a groan of her own. 'The only woman I couldn't satisfy was my wife.' One very revealing statement from a male of Damiano's sophistication and experience, she reflected in strong dismay.

'It didn't matter to me enough…I didn't understand,' she muttered in a tone of feverish regret, kissing a damp brown muscular shoulder in belated apology. She loved him so much. She had almost lost him. She was so hugely grateful that he had chosen to come back to her and give their marriage another chance.

'Past and forgotten,' Damiano assured her.

Suddenly she had a driving need to ask him if, as his family had insisted, he *had* considered divorcing her before he'd gone missing. But she hesitated and questioned whether she could handle a confirmation that would devastate her and add to her anxieties in the present. For if Damiano admitted that he had been on the brink of ditching her, wouldn't she now feel as though she was still on probation? No, some questions were better left unspoken.

Damiano snatched her from such thoughts by tugging her up out of concealment. Lustrous eyes smouldering like topaz in sunlight, he shifted fluidly beneath her, urging her into stirring contact with his renewed arousal. 'You know when I said that I wasn't going to fall on you like a sex-starved animal, I was being a wolf in sheep's clothing…I was lying my head off, *tesoro mio*,' Damiano confided thickly. 'I had been deprived for so long that not ripping off your clothes in the limo the first day was an act of remarkable restraint!'

'R-really?' Eden stammered hot-cheeked, helpless excitement gripping her as he crushed her parted lips hungrily under his, sending her senses reeling again with almost terrifying ease.

'I didn't want to risk scaring you into a fit... I intended to play a waiting game—'

'No more waiting,' she broke in urgently. 'No need for any games.'

All hot-blooded Italian male at that moment, Damiano surveyed her, patently revelling in the response she could neither conceal nor control and the dark flood of sensual pleasure already taking hold of her as he touched her.

About an hour later, having satiated them both on high-voltage sex, Damiano announced with admirable energy that he was hungry and rang for some food to be brought up.

'Service just like home...I take it,' Eden teased, catching the oversized towelling robe he tossed onto the bed for her use.

Damiano frowned. 'Obviously you didn't appreciate that kind of service...'

She stiffened at that note of censure. 'What do you mean?'

'Oh, come on...' Damiano said drily. 'You dump my name, walk out on my family and keep yourself by bloody sewing! You're a qualified teacher. If you had to work, why didn't you look for a teaching job more appropriate to your status?'

Eden had gone rigid. Tightening the robe into a waist-strangling knot, she scrambled off the bed, an angry flush mantling her face. 'You are such a snob!'

'Like hell I am!' Damiano launched at her. 'When you refused Nuncio's support, you were *also* rejecting everything that *I* ever gave you—'

'Your snobby name?' Rage had come out of nowhere to engulf Eden. She was so furious, she was shaking. 'Your ghastly family? What did you give me? A lot of jewellery and a flashy car and loads of credit cards and I was *miserable*!'

'Were you really?' Damiano purred between gritted white teeth.

'Yes, I was… I only stuck it out because I loved you!' Eden raged with clenched fists. 'Once you were gone, I could happily have lived in a hedge and worked as a tramp—'

'Tramps don't work,' Damiano inserted with cool, cutting logic.

'If I had gone for a teaching job, I would have had to explain who I was and there's something *you* don't understand. I doubt if I would have got the job. People treat you like a leper when your husband has gone missing—'

'Cut the melodrama,' Damiano advised witheringly.

'No, because you don't know what it was like for me. People haven't a clue what to say to a woman who was in my situation. They're also terrified that you're going to break down and embarrass them…although that type are preferable to the *other* sort who revel in every gruesome detail of your misery!' she flung at him. 'I wanted privacy and the only way I could have it was to set up a small business guaranteed not to attract attention.'

'So that you could star as the all-singing, all-dancing sewing version of the Little Match Girl?' Damiano drawled with silken scorn.

'I'll have you know that I'm making a darned good living!' Eden countered furiously. 'And I'll happily go back to it any time. Just you say the word!'

In the explosive silence that followed that threat a soft knock sounded on the door. Eden whipped round and stalked out through the French windows spread wide on the balcony outside. With trembling hands, she gripped the worn stone balustrade and stared out into the starry night. The lake far below reflected the pale crescent moon. She breathed in and shivered at the temper which had ripped up through her without warning. It was stress, she finally acknowledged. How could any woman be blissfully happy when she was being black-mailed and living in mortal terror of an exposure that might cost her the man she loved? She *had* to tell Damiano about Mark and Tina's affair within the next few days.

'At the press conference, there were a lot of cracks about how you chose to support yourself in my absence,' Damiano admitted from behind her.

Recalled from her frantic and fearful thoughts, Eden paled in dismay. 'The press already know where I was living...about the shop?'

'Evidently...come and get something to eat.' Damiano detached her death grip on the balustrade and stepped back again. 'Listen to me. Snobbery has nothing to do with this issue—'

'No?'

'No. What disturbs me is the fact that you so quickly rejected our whole life and everybody and everything connected with me. In my mind those are exactly the things to which I should have held fast in the same position.'

As he made that honest admission, tears of shame at

the truth she was refusing to tell him swam in her eyes. Had her position not become untenable with his hostile family, she would have chosen to stay in the town house. She whirled round into his strong arms like a homing pigeon. She drank in the warm, wonderfully familiar scent of him like an addict without hope of reclaim and muttered hoarsely, 'I'm sorry that you got embarrassed like that at the press conference—'

'*Dio mio, cara*... I'm not so sensitive. I have skin like a rhino after Montavia.' Damiano gazed down at her with sardonic amusement. 'Nothing short of the news that you had been working the streets to survive would have fazed me!'

Or that she had been blamed for having a torrid affair mere months after he had disappeared? Stifling that enervating thought, Eden let him usher her back indoors.

CHAPTER SIX

'I REALLY *do* want to know everything that happened to you in Montavia,' Eden murmured seriously.

His lean, strong face taut, Damiano studied her where she sat on the edge of a padded lounger by the side of the superb swimming pool. He hauled himself up out of the water with easy strength, wet and bronzed and stark naked. She blushed furiously, struggled to rescue her concentration, but his sheer magnificence challenged her hard.

It was mid-afternoon the next day and after a late and leisurely lunch they had finally dragged themselves out of the bedroom. She ached all over from the wildness of their lovemaking but there had been something even more precious about just *being* together even though they hadn't talked about anything in particular. And she knew that Damiano had felt that too for neither one of them had made the slightest effort to go to sleep in spite of their exhaustion.

Snatching up a fleecy towel, Damiano gave her a wry look of comprehension. 'The kidnapping is a long way back in the past for me, *cara*.'

'I'd still like to know...I *need* to know,' Eden persisted.

The quiet broken only by the background buzz of the crickets lingered.

'OK. In the first minute, my driver was killed in front of me,' Damiano delivered with grim abruptness, his hard bone-structure clenching, his eyes shadowing. 'I

113

was bundled into the back of a covered truck and beaten up. Standard stuff.'

Her tummy lurched with nausea and she lost colour. 'But why did these soldiers go after you in the first place? What did they hope to achieve?'

'Some total idiot decided that by holding me hostage they might magically get the previous government's loans written off.' Damiano's hard mouth twisted with derision at that fanciful belief. 'Then once I was taken, someone rather brighter realised that kidnapping an international banker would hardly impress the world with the new regime's credentials...or attract any further investment.'

She nodded jerkily, fighting not to think of him being beaten up but tears were burning the back of her eyes.

'Suddenly I was a liability, surplus to requirements. The only way I managed to stay alive until the camp was attacked was by persuading the commanding officer that I was so filthy rich, he could ransom me back to my family for his own personal profit,' Damiano revealed flatly.

She shuddered. 'And then you were hurt again—'

'When the rebel forces attacked, a grenade was thrown into the hut where I was being held. When I came round, I was being carted through the jungle on a pallet. Both my legs were broken...I was totally helpless and temporarily blinded by the explosion,' Damiano recalled with a grimace. 'I also had a fractured skull. But I acted a lot more confused than I was until I had come up with a credible identity with which to satisfy my rescuers that I was on their side. Then just when I had got mobile enough to make a covert break for the nearest border, the field hospital was overrun by government troops.'

'And then you dared not admit who you really were,' she completed heavily for him, recognising what a bitter source of frustration that must have been after he had gone through so much.

'The months after that were the toughest,' Damiano confided grimly. 'I spent a lot of time isolated in a punishment cell because I was always getting into fights.'

Eden gaped at him. 'Always getting into fights? *You?*'

Damiano dealt her an impatient look. 'Two of the guys I went in with were murdered by other inmates,' he told her flatly. 'I'd be dead if I hadn't learned to defend myself. By that stage, I was convinced I was going to spend the rest of my natural life locked up. For a while, I didn't much care *what* happened to me! It was months before we were sentenced for our supposed crimes against the state. Only then did I realise that I'd be released in a couple of years.'

Eden coiled her hands tightly together, feeling the full guilty weight of her own naivety about what it was like to live in such tough conditions. 'It must have been hell for you,' she mumbled, and the minute she'd said that she wished that she could have come up with something less inane.

But a long dark shadow fell over her. Damiano reached down and separated her trembling hands to tug her upright. His spectacular dark, deep-set eyes glittered with hard self-assurance. 'Montavia taught me to value what I have. *Not* to live in the past when I was damned lucky just to survive! I lost my freedom but I didn't lose anything that really mattered. And now that I am home, I will be ruthless in discarding anything I don't want from my life!'

Her eyes slid fearfully from his, tummy somersaulting at that blunt declaration of intent. What would he do when she told him about Mark and Tina? Whose story was Damiano most likely to believe? Hadn't Damiano always shown more faith in his family than he had shown in her? She had a horrendous vision of being ruthlessly discarded from Damiano's life in the way he had just mentioned. Damiano might not waste much time agonising over whether or not she might be guilty.

Nor could she easily forget all that the man from the Foreign Office had warned her about. What if Damiano's present desire for her *was* just a temporary thing? A transitional phase? He had never said that he loved her. Yet he cared about her and he still found her physically attractive. That latter combination wasn't a lot though, was it? How would she bear it if Damiano chose to walk away from her in a few weeks' time? And how much more likely was that development when he learnt about that wretched affair and his faith in her was tested?

'What's wrong?' Damiano asked, terrifyingly attuned it now seemed to her every change of mood.

'Nothing!' Thinking at frantic speed, she tilted her head to one side. 'I was actually wondering how you contrived to arrive here *ahead* of me last night. You never did explain that.'

'I walked out early on the board meeting at the bank.'

In considerable disconcertion, Eden stared at him.

'In five years the bank has had three different acting chairmen. With that many changes of policy, not to mention lax management, profits have dropped. They want me back in spite of the fact that I'm out of touch.' Damiano's expressive mouth curled. 'In fact they want me back like yesterday.'

'So...er, why did you leave the meeting early?'

His strong jawline squared. 'I saw no reason why I should allow myself to be put under pressure the instant I arrive home. The Braganzi Bank must wait.'

Eden swallowed hard on a statement which he would have once considered heresy. Once Damiano had *lived* for the Braganzi Bank, the cut and thrust of the money markets, the latest exciting and all-important deal. He had been a thriving workaholic who had taken twelve- to eighteen-hour working days in his stride. Damiano had sandwiched their marriage into the tiny spaces left over between appointments, trips abroad, late-night business powwows and a social life that had occupied several evenings a week.

'In about three weeks' time, I'll be attending another meeting in Rome. My Italian colleagues are possibly just a fraction more aware of what a man wants and needs after a long time away from his woman...' Damiano gazed down at her with a sudden outrageously wolfish grin, white teeth flashing, brilliant eyes full of self-mockery.

'Are they?' Her mouth ran dry and her heartbeat quickened. Beneath the onslaught of that teasing appraisal, that sexy assessing look he never made the slightest attempt to downplay, she felt as dizzy as a teenager. Damiano could shamelessly telegraph hot desire across a crowded room with a single lingering glance.

'Especially when the guy concerned is aware that his wife was once one of the most neglected wives in London—'

'But you used to notice me around bedtime—'

That charismatic grin merely slanted in easy acknowledgement of that direct hit. 'It didn't get me far, did it? You had me climbing walls in frustration—'

'But not any more,' she inserted in haste, struck afresh by the dangerous mistakes she had made during those early months of marriage. Such a gorgeous guy denied sex, made to feel unwelcome the one place he had had a right to feel welcome. Some men would have given up on her and strayed.

'You just made me want you more and more...' Damiano laughed throatily and grabbed her up into his arms, smouldering eyes raking over her heart-shaped face. 'In fact I don't mind admitting that, in the dark, you and your inseparable nightie gave me some incredibly exciting climaxes. There was always that aura of the forbidden to revel in. Not to mention the wonderful night I discovered that you were biting the pillow because you were so scared of making a noise. I suppose you didn't want to encourage me with the idea that you could be enjoying yourself that much—'

Cheeks aflame, she exclaimed, 'No...it was the knowledge that your sister, Cosetta, was in the room next door!'

In the very act of stepping down into the pool and lowering her into the shimmering turquoise water, Damiano stilled, sudden comprehension flaring in his spectacular dark golden eyes. 'Per amor di Dio...you were *that* self-conscious?' he groaned, all amusement vanquished as he caught her close to him. 'That never occurred to me. What a baby you still were...and you do choose your moments, don't you? Just when I was about persuade you out of your bikini and into rampant sex outdoors...'

Damiano's provocative drawl broke off at that precise moment, brows pleating at the clackety-clack noise of an approaching helicopter in the skies above. 'What the hell?' he began indignantly as if he owned the airspace as well as most of the land in sight.

A huge grin crept up to curve Eden's trembling mouth. 'And here you are stuck in the water naked as a jaybird. Suppose it's the paparazzi?' she whispered wickedly. 'I know you love risk, Damiano...but if Nuncio thought the shares might crash if you appeared in denim, what will happen if you appear in nothing but your skin?'

Even so, it was a shock to them both when the helicopter flew directly overhead and then began a descent on the far side of the villa. 'Visitors?' Eden yelped aghast.

Meshing one lean powerful hand into her hair, Damiano tipped her face up. 'You little witch,' he husked in a sexy growl, scanning her with hot, dark appreciative eyes and claiming her startled mouth in a devastatingly hungry kiss that wiped helicopters, visitors and even the fact she was standing in water right out of her mind.

Damiano lifted his head again, splaying his hands possessively over her bottom to urge her against his hotly aroused length. Then with an impatient curse in Italian, he set her back from him with pronounced reluctance. 'Who outside the family knows that we are here?'

It was some time before Eden discovered the answer to that salient question. While Damiano was able to dress at speed in the changing area by the pool and head straight off to greet their visitors, she had only a wrap to pull on over her wet bikini and had to rush upstairs to find clothes.

When she came down again, she walked straight into

the main salon, a grandiose state room furnished on a
princely scale with Brussels tapestries and magnificent
gilded furniture. Even Damiano had been thrown by the
sheer size of it when they had done a casual mini-tour
of the principal rooms on the ground floor the night
before. Immediately recognising the slim redhead seated
all by herself on a sofa, Eden hurried to greet the other
woman.

'Darcy? Why on earth are you sitting here on your
own?'

Rising to her feet, coolly elegant in a flowing turquoise dress, Darcy looked amused. 'Well, in the first
fine flush of male bonding, your husband and my husband just totally forgot about me. I've just seen them
walking along the terrace out there with drinks in their
hands!'

'Oh, dear…' Eden glanced in the direction of the
windows but the two men were no longer within view.

Darcy reached for Eden's hands with quiet but sincere warmth. 'I'm so happy for you and Damiano, Eden.
I cried my eyes out when I heard the news.' Her eyes
took on an apologetic light. 'And I'm afraid that Luca
just couldn't *wait* to see Damiano again.'

'I can understand that,' Eden said without hesitation
for the Italian banker, Luca Raffacani, was Damiano's
oldest friend. 'Did you bring the children with you?'

'Good heavens, no! I thought the two of us was quite
sufficient,' Darcy said ruefully. 'Five would have been
an invasion force!'

'Five…*five*?' Eden was doing basic sums and finally
appreciating just how long it had been since she had
seen the other couple. 'You've had another child? For
goodness' sake, of course, I'm really out of touch. Zia
must be eight now and we were at Pietro's christening

shortly before Damiano disappeared,' she recalled slowly.

'I had another little girl two years ago…look, Eden, that's not important,' Darcy countered, her delicate but vivid face looking troubled and serious. 'Do you remember the last time Luca called with you in London?'

'Yes, of course I do.' After Damiano had gone missing, Luca had visited her regularly when he'd been in London on business. However, Nuncio and Cosetta had always insisted on being present when anyone of Luca's importance had called and Eden had never got the chance to talk to Luca alone.

'Well, Luca was very disturbed by the way Damiano's brother and sister were treating you. He described the atmosphere as "poisonous",' Darcy confided with characteristic bluntness. 'We were going to ask you to come and stay with us but before we were able to *do* anything—'

'I'd left London and vanished without even mentioning what I was planning to do.' Eden's smile was strained as she attempted both to conceal her discomfiture at the direction in which the conversation was heading and stall it. Just how much *had* the formidably shrewd Luca Raffacani understood about what had been happening in the Braganzi family during that period? And was Darcy hinting that Luca might well bring Damiano up to speed on the same events?

'Luca made strenuous efforts to trace you.'

'That was very kind of him but I honestly managed fine, Darcy. I'm afraid I needed to come to terms with Damiano's disappearance on my own and I really wouldn't have wanted to inflict my misery on other people.' Eden used the distraction of lifting the phone to order refreshments. Her hand was trembling as she replaced the receiver.

'I've got this awful feeling that I've given you the wrong impression,' Darcy admitted anxiously. 'Luca and I just wish we had made a move sooner and done more to help before the situation got out of hand.'

'You did everything you possibly could and it was *very* much appreciated, believe me.' What situation? What was Darcy referring to? But, ironically, Eden was much too scared to ask. She suppressed her fears by telling herself that Luca Raffacani was far too clever and worldly wise to even consider making revelations which would cause trouble in a friend's marriage. 'But let's not look back. Right now, I can't help just wanting to revel in the fact that Damiano *has* come home to me.'

'Which is exactly as it should be,' Darcy agreed immediately, but her fine skin was flushed, her eyes now veiled. 'And in the normal way, I really would agree that family matters should stay strictly private *but*... Oh, dear, there I go again and Luca did warn me not to mention it!'

Eden took strength from that rueful admission and decided that it was highly unlikely that news of her supposed torrid affair nearly five years earlier had travelled as far afield as Italy. She really was getting paranoid! A single story by one British tabloid newspaper would scarcely have made news round the world, she scolded herself. She gave her outspoken companion a sympathetic smile. 'Have you ever noticed that the minute you're warned not to say something, it's the one thing that you can't get out of your mind?'

'Isn't it *just*?' Pushing back her springy auburn curls from her brow, Darcy relaxed at that rejoinder and laughed. 'I'm no good at keeping things in but Luca is wonderfully discreet!'

Receiving that as a reassuring declaration, Eden recalled how envious she had once been of the strength of Luca and Darcy's happy marriage. Such different personalities yet they complemented each other: Darcy so guileless and down-to-earth, Luca, infinitely more complex and reserved. The two women walked along the terrace, taking in the wonderful views of the Tuscan countryside drowsing in the afternoon heat and eventually found Luca and Damiano.

Both men interrupted their keen conversation to glance at their wives with the slightly wary expressions of males belatedly recalling their existence. Eden was tense until Luca Raffacani greeted her with a lazy smile, his legendary reserve nowhere in evidence with friends. Damiano dropped his arm round Eden and drew her possessively close, the heat and proximity of his sun-warmed body soothing the last of her concerns and firing a glow of happiness in her eyes. In times gone by, Damiano would not have been so demonstrative in front of other people.

Eden watched Luca tug at a strand of Darcy's tumbling pre-Raphaelite curls, his wife's answering smile up into her husband's eyes. And then she found Damiano looking down at her, his burnished golden gaze pinned to her tense face, a slight frown-line drawing his expressive dark brows together. The memory of that rather questioning look stayed with her.

The conversation roved on to the theatrical grandeur of the Villa Pavone which had been restored right down to the smallest detail. Damiano explained that his late grandmother, Livia Braganzi, had left architectural historians in charge of the project. 'They had four years in which to complete their work—'

'And the only power showers are in the pool complex,' Eden chipped in with amusement, recalling Damiano's comical horror in the early hours when he had gone into the massive *en suite* bathroom to take a shower and found only a giant bath in the shape of a clam shell.

'So there's still a few improvements to be made because I have no intention of living *in* the eighteenth century,' Damiano commented feelingly. 'We have a pool only because *Nonna* was a keen swimmer.'

'Your grandmother brought you and your siblings up after your parents died, didn't she?' Darcy prompted Damiano with interest. 'To manage that *and* devote her life to restoring historic buildings, she must have been a very active woman.'

Only a great deal less active in the parenting stakes, Eden reflected inwardly. Livia Braganzi had been an extremely rich intellectual. Widowed with only one child while she was still a young woman, she had been obsessed by her restoration projects and not remotely maternal. Damiano's parents had died in a car crash when he was thirteen. His grandmother had idolised him, he had once admitted to Eden, purely because he was so clever. His brother and sister had fared less well against that demanding yardstick of approval. Damiano's protective attitude towards his siblings had been fostered from an early age.

Pressed to do so, Darcy and Luca stayed to dinner before taking their leave.

'Why were you uncomfortable with Luca?' Damiano enquired within minutes of the departure of their guests.

They were sitting over fresh coffee in the picturesque

vine-covered loggia watching the sun sink down behind the hills. Eden flushed and tried not to stiffen. 'Was I?'

'Initially noticeably ill at ease, then you seemed to relax.' His lean, strong face taut, Damiano studied her with cool condemnation. 'It bothers me that I should have to hear from someone else what I should have been told by you.'

To mask her growing nervous tension, Eden had begun stirring her coffee, and, so stricken was she by what Damiano was saying, she kept on stirring as though her life depended on it. The *affair*…it had to be that he was talking about! She could feel the blood draining from her features, the sudden clamminess of her skin, the sick sensation of foreboding turning her tummy queasy.

'*Dio mio*…I am genuinely grateful that Luca chose to be so frank with me,' Damiano continued, his hard mouth ruthlessly cast. 'Why couldn't *you* tell me that, virtually from the moment of my disappearance, my family began treating you like dirt?'

At that revealing question which told her that her guilty conscience had provoked near panic far in advance of any true threat, Eden's head jerked up. 'Well…er, I—'

Anger now clearly evident in his splintering dark gaze, Damiano rammed back his chair and rose to his full commanding height. 'Luca said he noticed their hostility towards you the very first time he visited. He said my sister embarrassed you in front of the staff by countermanding your instructions and indeed went out of her way to stress that *she* was the hostess in what was *your* home!'

'It was always like that when you weren't around,' Eden admitted grudgingly.

Damiano stared at her in complete shock. She saw

that he had listened to what Luca had said but had undoubtedly hoped that Luca had somehow misinterpreted what he had seen during his visits to the town house. 'Even *before* I went missing?' he emphasised rawly.

Eden sighed and then nodded.

'Yet you never uttered a single word of complaint!' Damiano surveyed her with thunderous incredulity.

'You told me that your family was the most important thing in your life. Furthermore, the last thing a new wife wants to do is to start criticising her husband's relatives when she *has* to live with them,' Eden responded flatly. 'I'm afraid they had got used to the idea of you marrying Annabel and I was a very unwelcome surprise.'

'But Tina, at least, was your friend…'

'*Not* if it was likely to bring her into conflict with Nuncio or Cosetta. Tina would never cross Cosetta. That's how she keeps the peace.'

Deprived of even the comfort of believing that his sister-in-law had been supportive, Damiano expelled his breath in a stark kiss. 'I understand that Nuncio implied within Luca's hearing that it was somehow your fault that I had gone to Montavia.'

Eden gave a second reluctant nod of affirmation.

'*Porca miseria!*' Damiano exclaimed in outrage. 'How the hell could my own brother make such a ridiculous charge against you?'

Eden paled. 'Your brother and your sister were aware that our marriage was under strain before you left. They believed that if you had been more happily married you would have let one of the bank executives make that trip.'

Damiano was now white with rage below his bronzed complexion. '*Accidenti!* To say such a thing to my wife when she was grieving for me was unforgivable!'

'Damiano…when you went missing, everybody went haywire,' Eden tried to explain gently. 'But, let's face it, I should have stood up for myself long before that happened. Instead I let your family walk all over me and sat feeling sorry for myself, rather than *doing* something about the situation.'

'Do not attempt to excuse them for their appalling behaviour!' Damiano grated. 'You were my *wife*—'

'Yes, but—'

'My wife, who stood to inherit everything I possessed once I was officially declared dead. No doubt that in itself made you a target for their resentment,' Damiano interposed, settling on mercenary motives for his family's attitude with a cynical speed that shook Eden. 'Forgive me for *ever* questioning your refusal to accept my brother's financial support!'

'Don't go over the top about this.' Dismayed by his attitude, Eden got up from her chair. 'Your brother and sister were devastated by your disappearance and their distress *was* genuine—'

'*Santo Cielo*…how could I have been so blind?' Damiano demanded abruptly, his brilliant dark eyes bleak. 'How much did my *own* thoughtless behaviour contribute to what you suffered at their hands?'

'Don't make such a big deal of it now,' Eden urged, seeing no benefit to anyone in his fury so long after the event. 'As long as you never ask me to live with them again, I can let bygones be bygones.'

'You are much too forgiving and generous, *tersoro mio*. There will, nevertheless, be a calling to account,' Damiano delivered with grim assurance. 'I will not let this matter die. Indeed, I cannot. I trusted my family to look after you when I could not be there for you.'

'But I didn't need looking after,' Eden protested.

Damiano pulled her into his arms, crushing her into the heat and solidity of his big powerful frame with strong hands. 'I'd have gone mad in Montavia if I had known that you were being victimised and hurt by those closest to me!' he bit out in a still wrathful undertone above her head.

'I *still* would prefer you to let all this stay buried. Everybody's been upset enough and I do wish Luca Raffacani had minded his own business!'

'Since it's obvious you weren't going to tell me, I'm glad *he* had the sense to do so,' Damiano countered without hesitation. '*Dio mio*…one needs to know who one can trust.'

That phrase sent a stabbing little chill down Eden's spine. Would Damiano still trust her if he knew what she was keeping to herself? And then her eyes flashed angrily as she registered the astonishing level of her own guilt. What had she done? *Nothing!* It was time she reminded herself of that fact. Why shouldn't she protect their wonderful togetherness from all malign influences? Why should *she* have to make an awkward explanation about the sordid scandal which Tina and Mark had selfishly created? Well, she would tell Damiano when she was good and ready and in the meantime? In the meantime, she was determined not to allow that business to hang over her like an executioner's axe, filling her with fear and unease as it had this afternoon when Darcy had spoken rather too frankly.

Damiano anchored his hands round her and lifted her high. A wry smile chased the remnants of anger from his lean, strong face. 'You look *really* cross with me—'

'Not with *you*.' Her heart in her eyes, Eden gazed

down at him with helpless tenderness. 'With Luca for laying all that on you now.'

Damiano strode indoors with his arms still firmly wrapped round her. 'I was surprised but evidently what he witnessed left a deep impression on him. I dare say he was shocked. However, I'm tough, *cara mia*. Why do we have to trek a mile to get to our bedroom in this house?' he lamented, lowering her slowly down the length of his taut, muscular physique, catching her up again halfway through that manoeuvre to take her lips with passionate hunger.

She clung to him with feverish force, stretching up on tiptoe to let her fingers plunge into his springy black hair and hold him close. Her body was coming alive all on its own. He was kissing her with the same deep, driving sensuality with which he made love. He fired a tide of hot, quivering longing that made her breasts ache and her thighs tremble. He sank down on a gilded chair that creaked in alarming complaint beneath their combined weight.

Dragging his mouth from hers, he got up again in haste and vented a rueful laugh. 'Right, you can put the twee dainty chairs into storage for starters. I'll choose comfort over authenticity any day!'

'One, power shower,' she whispered, utterly dazzled by his glorious smile, heart racing to such an extent she could hardly catch her breath. 'Two, chairs to do *more* than sit in—'

'Did I say that?' Damiano asked mockingly as he headed for the stairs.

'For once, I'm ahead of you.'

'And without the vodka too—'

Eden reddened and mock-punched a broad shoulder. 'That was low—'

'No, low would be discussing the episode in depth and telling you that I really do wish that I had kept my mouth shut five minutes longer...' Damiano regarded her with smouldering eyes and a thoroughly wicked grin '...just to see what you had planned for me—'

'Damiano—'

'Instead of which I blew a gasket but you can blame Ramon Alcoverro for that development,' Damiano informed her without warning. 'Do you know what Ramon said very quietly to me one minute before I left Brazil?'

Eden frowned in bewilderment as Damiano lowered her down onto their bed. 'No...what?'

'"Your wife's been playing away...thought I should mention it since your little brother didn't have the guts!" Bastard!' Damiano ground out feelingly, adding something in Italian that sounded extremely derogatory, mercifully not looking at her as he slipped off her shoes. 'So I had the entire flight back to London to wonder about what I was coming home to and work out this trite little speech about how I understood if there had been other guys...like *hell* would I have understood!'

Eden closed her shattered eyes and now remembered how incredibly tense Damiano had been with her those first few minutes at the airfield. 'I—'

'*Sì*...I agree. That is a totally unreasonable attitude considering that you spent a good four and a half years of your life thinking you were a widow,' Damiano conceded, into full, unstoppable flow now on a subject which had patently disturbed him a great deal. 'But a guy who's been caged like an animal for the same length of time is *not* reasonable, I assure you. I put you on a pedestal like a little saint. I couldn't bear even to consider the idea that you might have slept with another man—'

Eden sidled back into the shadows cast by the bed curtains. She was pale as death.

Damiano breathed in deep, shimmering dark eyes full of raw emotion as he came down on the edge of the bed. 'If I had lost you, I would have felt as if I had lost *everything,*' he confessed with roughened urgency. 'I had so much faith in you...but I was very scared that Ramon might be telling me the truth!'

It was the moment when she should have spoken up, explained why Ramon had said such a thing. Evidently that nasty little tabloid story had travelled as far as Brazil in terms of gossip at the least. But she lay there like a stone on a riverbed resisting the force of the current and said unevenly, 'Would you have divorced me?'

'Shush...' Damiano scolded with a wince at the sound of that word and he lifted her hand, spread her fingers and pressed his lips almost reverently to her palm. Then he raised his handsome dark head and surveyed her with immense appreciation. 'I may not have respected your moral scruples before we got married, *cara mia*...but I clung to my memory of them every day I was in prison.'

'Hmm...' Eden's voice was so small it was practically inaudible. 'Would you have divorced me?'

'What is this preoccupation with that subject?'

'I'm...I'm just curious,' she mumbled half under her breath.

Sì...probably,' Damiano groaned in frustration at her persistence. 'Out of pride and jealousy and pain. Now you're annoyed with me, aren't you?'

Eden had flipped away from him onto her side. 'No!'

With a throaty chuckle, Damiano tugged her relent-

lessly back into his arms. 'Don't you know how much
I need you?' he husked, stringing out a teasing line of
kisses across her sealed lips. 'Now, I've never told any
woman that before—'

Involuntarily, a smile crept up on her tense mouth.
'*So* macho—'

In the midst of that sentence, he brought his mouth
down with sexy provocative heat on hers and she knew
she hadn't spoken when she should have spoken but,
once he had said that about divorce, she knew she just
couldn't take that big a risk. She would tell him before
they left Italy and returned to London, she promised
herself. Chain him to a wall first, lock every exit, she
told herself fancifully.

Over three weeks later, Eden strolled through the wild
woodland at the lower end of the Villa Pavone's ter-
raced gardens. Damiano had been away for thirty-six
hours in Rome. He had asked her to accompany him
but she had said no. Saying no had cost her but they
had spent endless days and nights solely together and
intelligence had warned her that it was time to stand
back and not cling like a neurotic.

This time, Damiano was going to come home. In her
head she knew that but she hadn't slept a wink the night
before because there was no common sense to be found
in her heart. She missed him so much, she was counting
the hours and minutes still to be got through. He was
due home in the evening. He had phoned her several
times. Once in the middle of the night to complain that
he kept on waking up because she wasn't there. She
had oozed sympathy but she had liked that—oh, yes,
she had liked that, wouldn't have been at all happy if
he had slept like a log without her.

Damiano was more hers than he had ever been. Damiano was treating her like the most precious and wonderful woman in the world. It seemed that losing each other had taught them to value each other more and value pride a great deal less. And, of course, loving him to bits helped. Not to mention the mutually insatiable passion which she no longer felt threatened by. Indeed, she thought, feeling a slight flush warm her face, she was pretty shameless in that department now. Well, in *her* estimation, she was. Almost every problem resolved...just the one left.

However, it did take courage to face up to the nasty necessity of finally telling Damiano about Mark and Tina's affair and the consequences she had foolishly brought down on herself. But, Eden reflected anxiously, it had to be done. Tiring of the shaded walk, she wandered off it into the sunlit maze between towering dark hedges as impenetrable as walls. Would she be able to find her way to the centre without Damiano's superior sense of direction as guidance?

'Ed-en!'

A huge smile of surprise flashed across her face as she recognised that distant call. Evidently, Damiano had returned from Rome sooner than he had expected. She yelled back and cursed the fact that she had gone into the maze. Excitement had caused her to lose her bearings and, absurdly, she had to keep on shouting.

It was ironic that while she was attempting to find the fastest way out again, she instead found herself on a one-way path and ended up at the centre of the maze instead. The fabulous fountain there shot sprays of glittering water high into the hot still air. 'I'm at the fountain!' she called with a grin and the knowledge that she would never let on that she had arrived there accidentally.

'*Per amor di Dio*...I am not in the mood for some stupid game!'

That comeback made Eden flush in disconcertion. But then possibly he was tired and had been searching the extensive gardens for longer than patience could bear. About thirty seconds later, she heard his footsteps crunch on the gravel surface within the maze. 'I'm not playing a game...it's just I thought you could come in quicker than I would find my way out!' she announced on a note of apology.

Just ten feet away from her, Damiano strode suddenly into view. He stopped dead then as though a repelling forcefield surrounded her. And he looked at her as he had never in his life looked at her. With seething anger and derision and hatred. And *that* quickly, Eden knew, long before he spoke, even before he flung the newspaper cutting in his hand, that she had waited far *too* long to tell him that story...

CHAPTER SEVEN

THE newspaper cutting fluttered down onto the sunlit gravel. Eden gave the crumpled snap of Tina and Mark's torrid embrace only a brief and pained glance.

'It is your deliberate deception that disgusts me most!' Damiano breathed in a stupendously quiet assurance that nonetheless cut through the surging silence like a whiplash. 'At every opportunity when you might have spoken up, you chose to lie.'

'No, I haven't told you any lies,' Eden murmured tautly, snatching in a breath of the hot, still air, perspiration dampening her upper lip. 'It was Tina who had the affair with Mark. That is Tina, *not me*, in that photograph, Damiano—'

'*Accidenti!* I'm not listening to nonsense like that—'

Eden's pale face tightened. 'Well, while you're not listening, would you please tell me where you got that cutting from?'

His aggressive jawline clenched. 'Yet another one of the well-wishers who appear to surround me but, on this occasion, an anonymous one. That tabloid trash was delivered to me by special courier this morning. It was sent from London.'

Eden was fighting to keep calm, fighting to stay in control and not give way to the reality that she was weak with shock. 'Probably by Tina. Now that she views me as a threat, she's keen to see me drummed out of the family. If you think about this awful business calmly—'

'*Calmly?*' Damiano derided thickly as if he was having difficulty even getting that word out, but volume-wise he was doing very well.

'I swear that I have never been intimate with Mark. We haven't ever even kissed. It was always a platonic friendship...'

Ashen below his bronzed skin, Damiano continued to stare at her with unreadable fixity, eyes black as obsidian, stunningly handsome features as inflexible as a stone carving.

Knowing as surely as if he had told her that he was recalling that she had once admitted to having had a teenage crush on Mark, Eden trembled and set off hurriedly on another track. It was dreadful that her mind should let her down in the midst of such a confrontation. But panic had such a grip on her, she couldn't get her teeming thoughts in order or even work out quite where to begin to tell her side of what had happened almost five years earlier.

'I didn't *know* Mark and Tina were having an affair until the story broke in that newspaper,' she told him tautly. 'Mark visited the town house a great deal those first weeks after you were missing. He and Tina got on well but I never thought anything of that...I mean, why would I? I was too wrapped up in my own misery to be that observant. Tina began to suggest that we went down to the country house at Oxford at weekends. Mark was still working there then—'

'You're wasting your time with this,' Damiano drawled lethally. 'I lost my freedom, not my brain, in South America.'

Eden just kept on talking for, now that she had begun, she could not stop the words spilling out. 'We would drive down in my car. Tina said it was good for me to have to do something that I had to think about and she was probably right…I was like a zombie then. She left me alone a lot those weekends but it never occurred to me that she was with Mark. I wasn't much company, so I wasn't surprised when she would say she was off to visit friends and she took my car…where are you going?' she gasped as Damiano simply swung on his heel and started to walk back into the maze.

'You're telling me lies a child could tear apart. Mark was *your* friend. Mark was *your* constant visitor. Mark was living down on our country estate purely because *you* insisted that I employ him. But then you always had to keep Mark within reach. Why the hell did you marry *me*?'

Eden unfroze from her stupor and raced after him. 'How on earth can you ask me that?'

Damiano stilled without turning back to her, broad shoulders taut with savage tension beneath the fine cloth of his charcoal-grey jacket. 'I don't trust my temper…I don't want to continue this pointless dialogue—'

'You owe it to me to hear me out!' Eden broke in incredulously.

'I don't owe you anything now…' Damiano vented a sudden raw and bitter laugh that made her shiver. 'But thanks for a few memorable lays.'

'Just you turn round and say that to my face!' Eden launched at him shakily.

Unexpectedly, Damiano did swing back. 'Do you know what I really thought was wrong with our marriage before I went to Montavia?'

Eden folded her arms jerkily, her legs trembling beneath her. 'No.'

'Mark…every which way I turned, I came on Mark! You seemed much closer to him that you were to me,'

Damiano delivered grittily, black eyes beginning to take on a stormy glitter of gold, the determinedly level drawl now harshening. 'Naturally I resented him; naturally I was jealous of him—'

'J-jealous?' Eden stammered with a sinking sensation in the pit of her stomach for that was something, and a very dangerous something, which she had never once suspected.

'Remarkable that, isn't it? That *I* should have been jealous of a weak, unscrupulous little jerk, who was openly out for everything he could get? Do you think Mark would have been such an attentive friend if you had married a poor man? He played you like a violin, Eden. I had to stand back and watch it!'

Every syllable of that contemptuous and humiliatingly accurate assessment of Mark's character bit deep into Eden's shrinking flesh. Damiano had seen what she had not. Just a few weeks ago, she would have loyally defended Mark. Now the knowledge that she had allowed Mark to blackmail her weighed her down with a numbing sense of her own inadequacy.

Damiano studied her with hard, biting derision, dark, deep-set eyes frighteningly bleak. 'When my family turned against you after I went missing, Mark must have seemed like your only refuge. Presumably that's how you ended up in bed with him,' he breathed in a chilling assumption that shook her rigid. 'Did you then tell yourself that you were in love with him?'

Eden was aghast at that question and even more by the reasoning he had employed, explaining to his own apparent satisfaction how she might have succumbed to such an affair. Registering that her efforts to defend herself had so far made no impression whatsoever on

Damiano, she exclaimed, 'I didn't end up in bed with Mark! I swear I didn't!'

His lean, powerful face grim, Damiano appraised her with embittered contempt. Swinging on his heel, he strode off, feet crunching on the gravel. The sun beating down on her, Eden stayed where she was, in so much shock she could not immediately react.

Damiano had sent her reeling with revelations of his own. She saw now that she was in much deeper trouble than she could ever have imagined. Damiano had *always* been jealous of her attachment to Mark! Jealous to the level of having once believed that her fondness for the younger man was threatening their marriage. For a split second she could have screamed her frustration to the skies for Damiano had carefully concealed that jealousy from her. And now circumstances had combined horribly to construct a scenario which Damiano appeared to find disturbingly credible. He was quite prepared to believe that, in the fraught aftermath of his own disappearance, she had turned to Mark for more than the comfort of friendship.

So hot that her dress was now sticking to her damp skin, Eden found her way out of the maze. Now she couldn't believe she had been so stupid as to allow Damiano to walk away from her. In panic she raced through the beautiful gardens, heart thumping like a crazed drumbeat driving her on. She had to climb two long flights of stone steps to reach the terrace at the rear of the villa. She sped indoors, dizzy from exertion and frantic with fear that Damiano might already have swung back into his limo and departed.

When she found Damiano in the library which he had begun using as an office soon after their arrival, she fell still in the doorway, breasts rising and falling as she struggled just to catch her breath again. Relief filled her to overflowing in those first taut seconds.

His lean, strong-boned features savagely taut, Damiano sent her a dark look of scorching aggression. 'Get out,' he said softly, a slight tremor marring his usual even diction.

'Not until you give me the chance to defend myself.'

Damiano gave a great shout of sardonic laughter. 'Defend yourself? Who are you trying to kid? Do you think I don't appreciate what's been going on around me since I came home? Everybody *but* me knew that you had had an affair!'

'But I didn't have an affair!' Eden flung back at him wildly.

'Now I understand why Nuncio did not bring you to Brazil. Now I know why you ditched my name and went into hiding. You were embarrassed and ashamed—'

'No, I was just fed up with your family and the whole stupid mess I'd landed myself in! I only made *one* mistake, Damiano. When the press erroneously identified the woman in that photograph as me, I was faced with a very difficult choice,' Eden insisted in growing desperation as she moved deeper into the room, her whole concentration bent on him. 'If I spoke up and pointed out that that woman was Tina, I was going to wreck her marriage and she begged me to keep quiet—'

'Tell me, how long did it take you to come up with this melodramatic tale in which you were the only victim and *every* member of my family was rotten to the core?' Damiano slashed back at her in unconcealed disgust.

'Tina said it was my fault that her affair with Mark

was exposed and, in a twisted way, she was right,' Eden conceded shakily.

'What are you trying to say?'

'That there wouldn't have *been* a story if that paparazzo photographer hadn't assumed that that woman kissing Mark was me! And my only claim to fame was being the wife of a well-known banker who had gone missing in a huge shower of publicity. That was what made me a target and that was what made that story of my supposed infidelity worth printing!'

'I am never going to believe that someone as prim and proper as you used to be agreed to be labelled an adulteress for Tina's benefit!' With that seething proclamation of disbelief, Damiano strode past her, long, powerful strides carrying him towards the stairs at a far faster rate than she could emulate.

'All right, what I did was downright stupid but you should know me better!' Eden protested as she hurried breathlessly up the stairs in his stormy wake. 'I thought you were dead. I was trying to cope with my own grief. I really didn't *want* to feel responsible for Tina losing Nuncio as well!'

With a ground-out exclamation in Italian, Damiano fell still on the landing, his lean hands clenching into powerful fists. 'Stop this *now*! Where is your dignity?'

'When have I *ever* lied to you?' Eden demanded rawly.

She looked up at him. He looked back down at her. The atmosphere was thick with sizzling undertones. She collided with his stunning dark golden eyes and finally saw the tremendous pain he was attempting to hide from her, the savage restraint he was exerting over his emotions.

Eden trembled, tummy churning. She sensed that she

had finally said something that penetrated, something he was finally prepared to consider.

The silence hung like a giant weight ready to fall.

Damiano's black spiky lashes lowered, eyes narrowing to glittering pinpoints of ferocious intensity. 'You have never had cause to lie to me before.'

Eden flinched as if he had struck her, the feverish colour in her cheeks draining away, 'And you have *never* trusted me,' she muttered in a stricken tone of discovery. 'Evidently you didn't even trust me when we were first married. What did I ever do to deserve that?'

Dark blood scored the high cheekbones which stood out with such chiselled prominence below Damiano's bronzed skin. He said nothing.

Eden mounted the remaining stairs until they were level, the shock and hurt in her eyes unconcealed. 'You hid so much from me five years ago…I had no idea that you resented Mark. I really didn't understand what I was dealing with until now.' Her throat aching with unshed tears, Eden turned away. 'That's, it, then, isn't it? Because I don't have any proof of my innocence to offer you!'

As she headed down the corridor to their bedroom, a lean hand suddenly snapped round her wrist, staying her. Damiano scanned her strained, tear-wet face with savage dark golden eyes. 'What do you mean, "That's it"?'

Eden pulled free of him in an equally abrupt movement. Even though she was shaking like a leaf and starting to feel rather dizzy, she thrust up her chin in challenge. 'Well, what do you think I mean?'

Eyes a scorching, aggressive gold, Damiano growled, 'No way are you leaving me!'

Thoroughly confused by that assurance when she had

assumed *he* was set on walking out and leaving *her*, Eden blinked. 'B-but—'

'You tell me the truth and I'll attempt to put this matter behind us.' Damiano gritted out each word of that promise as if it physically hurt.

Eden was so taken aback she simply gaped at him.

'The *truth*,' Damiano emphasised.

'But you won't believe me.'

'Maybe you never actually went as far as *sleep* with him...maybe I could believe that,' Damiano ground out thinly between clenched teeth, misinterpreting what she had said.

Eden tilted her pounding head to one side, wishing that annoying dizziness afflicting her would recede, and looked at him in increasing bewilderment. 'You really don't know *what* to believe, do you?' A great weariness engulfed her then. 'And I can do nothing but tell you the rest of the story. Tina and I discussed this in London. She has already said that she will lie to protect herself...and Mark is only willing to tell the truth for a price.'

Damiano frowned down at her without comprehension. 'A price?'

'He said he'd throw his lot in with Tina and lie if I didn't give him money,' Eden mumbled sickly. 'Mark is blackmailing me, Damiano.'

Wrenching open the door, Eden fled into the bedroom. One glimpse of Damiano's transfixed expression was sufficient to make her slam the door. With her emotional turmoil at a level beyond what she could handle, making that final confession had made her feel marginally better. She had finally told him the entire truth.

Only a full two minutes *after* making that admission did
her intelligence kick back in and shriek that she should
have kept quiet about the blackmail. Now Damiano
would be absolutely convinced of her guilt!

CHAPTER EIGHT

EDEN listened to the silence. Damiano did not follow her into the bedroom.

Still feeling dizzy and absently wondering whether stress could make one feel *that* light-headed, she flung herself on the bed and cried until there were no tears left. By then her eyes were sore and puffy and she was hot and exhausted. Pulling off her crumpled clothing, she crawled into the bed. Then she lay there dully wondering what to do next.

Was she supposed to be pleased that Damiano evidently cared enough about their marriage to declare that he would try to put her apparent infidelity behind him? What she did appreciate was how little she had once been able to read the volatile male whom she had married. Damiano jealous of Mark? It was as if Damiano had never ever quite been able to bring himself to believe that she loved him...why?

Somewhere in the midst of trying to work out that mystery while trying not to succumb to an urge to go and search the villa to see if Damiano was still in residence, Eden fell asleep. When she opened her eyes again, the room was dimly lit. She moved her head experimentally and was relieved that that strange dizziness had receded. She turned over then and got a shock.

Damiano was sprawled in an armchair only about a foot away. Jacket and tie discarded, black hair tousled, he had not followed his usual habit of shaving a second time in the evening. A definable blue-black shadow of stubble outlining his formidable jawline, he was nursing a brandy goblet between his lean hands while he studied her from below lush ebony lashes with keen intensity.

'Wh-what?' she stammered unsteadily, unnerved by that scrutiny.

Damiano loosed a heavy sigh and stretched his big shoulders back. 'I want to hear about Mark trying to blackmail you,' he admitted.

Tensing up even more, Eden paled and stared at him in bewilderment. 'I...I gave him the money—'

All apparent relaxation abandoned, Damiano leapt up like a lion about to spring, an expression of unholy disbelief etched on his tough features. 'You did...*what*?'

Eden gulped and sat up, clutching the sheet to her quaking frame. 'He threatened to support Tina's story instead. What was I supposed to do? How do you think you would have reacted to all this coming out within days of you getting home? I wanted time with you...I didn't want everything ruined—'

'You do realise that you are damning yourself more with every word you say?' Damiano cut in flatly.

'But it *is* the truth I'm telling you,' Eden insisted. 'I was scared of the damage Mark might do if he got together with Tina, so I gave Mark all the money I had in my bank account when he asked for it—'

An expression of shaken fascination stamping his lean, strong face, Damiano sank down heavily on the edge of the bed. 'You just *gave* him it...how much?' he practically whispered.

After chewing at her lower lip for a second or two, she surrendered and told him. 'I thought our marriage was worth it,' she muttered heavily.

'That is a highly original excuse for paying a blackmailer,' Damiano conceded grittily, his broad chest swelling as he breathed in very deep as if he was having a hard time controlling his temper. 'Anstey demanded the money the day you flew out here, didn't he?'

She gave a jerky nod and swallowed hard.

'That creepy little bastard!' Damiano condemned with a sudden vicious force that made her flinch.

'I'm sorry…I'm so sorry about *all* of this!' Eden sobbed, flopping down to push her face wretchedly into the pillows.

'Console yourself with the thought that by the time I'm finished some people are going to be a great deal sorrier,' Damiano imparted darkly, and he went on to ask further detailed questions concerning Mark. But Eden had few concrete answers to offer. She knew Mark's mobile phone number but not his current address and was unsure of the exact location of the organic farm company at which she understood he worked.

She heard Damiano stand up again and she lifted her head. 'I never would have slept with Mark,' she swore in a vehement rush. 'I couldn't imagine doing that with anybody but you.'

'That does have a certain ring of veracity, *cara mia*. Sadly, however, the vodka incident you treated me to the first day doesn't do much to support your case,' Damiano admitted bluntly. 'To me that now looks very much like you overcompensating out of a massive guilt complex.'

Eden looked at him with reddened eyes now finally beginning to spark with angry resentment. 'Right…just you go on thinking that. Just you go right on rationalising your conviction that I'm guilty. Frankly, I think I've had enough grief over something I didn't do!'

In the rushing silence which followed, Damiano shed his shirt.

Eden bounced up against the pillows, no longer limp and weepy. 'What do you think you're doing?'

Unzipping his tailored trousers, Damiano gave her a level glance. 'I'm coming to bed—'

'You're not coming to bed with me!' Eden declared in angry astonishment. 'You don't believe me about Mark... So you can go and sleep somewhere else!'

At a leisurely pace, Damiano removed the remainder of his clothing. Naked and unconcerned, he strolled back across the room.

'OK...you can sleep here if you must.' Eden withdrew her objections just as suddenly as she had made them for she recalled with a shiver of foreboding just how much of a distance separate bedrooms had imposed between them in the distant past.

'*Grazie,*' Damiano purred in liquid Italian.

'You're not thinking of a divorce, then?' As the lights went out, that demand just erupted from her and she cringed, embarrassed by her lack of control over her own tongue.

'Not just at the moment, no,' Damiano drawled flatly. 'But I'm probably going to make your life hell while I try to come to terms with this.'

'Is that a threat?'

'A warning.'

In the darkness tears welled up again and stung her eyes. He didn't believe her; he was *never* going to believe that she hadn't betrayed him with Mark.

In an abrupt movement, Damiano closed lean hands to her waist and tugged her across the great divide between them into his arms. Nervous as a cat, Eden vented a startled gasp.

'I still want you, *cara,*' he breathed rawly.

Now in intimate contact with his lean, muscular physique, Eden was in no doubt of the truth of that claim, but she was taken aback. 'But you—'

'I'm not so sensitive,' Damiano growled. 'And you can't afford to be.'

Flung into disarray by that uncompromising approach, Eden quivered against him, the heat and hunger of him striking her at every treacherous pulse-point.

'Damiano—?'

'You want me too. The love might be fake but the sex is *real*,' Damiano spelt out raggedly. 'And I'm quite happy to settle for a great time in bed right now.'

Those words hurt her so much but she was painfully aware that he was hurting too and she blamed herself entirely for that. But so strained and unhappy did she feel that she genuinely believed she would not be able to respond. And then Damiano crushed her mouth under his with demanding hunger. It was a considerable shock for Eden to find herself not only responding but clinging with a kind of desperate fervour way beyond anything she had expected to feel.

'You're *my* wife…' Damiano spelt out, releasing her swollen lips and then delving them apart with the invasive eroticism of his tongue before she could reply.

He sent such a jolt of sensual excitement leaping through her, she gasped beneath that onslaught. And so it went on. The stroke of his hand across her breast followed by the urgency of his mouth on the aching peak, arching her spine off the bed, making her cry out. By the time he discovered the moist readiness at the heart of her, she was way beyond control, possessed by a frantic intensity of need and excitement combined.

And then, without any warning at all, Damiano was suddenly thrusting her back from him, gritting out something savage in Italian. A split second later, Eden was sitting up in shock. In the shadowy path of the moonlight filtering into the room, she watched Damiano vault off the bed and stride into the bathroom. With an unsteady hand, she switched on the lights. She listened to the power shower he had had installed running at full force.

Shattered by his last-minute rejection of her, she got up, pulled on a light robe and sank down in the chair he had vacated earlier. Her body ached and she hated it for aching for she knew that what had just transpired was infinitely more important than any transitory pleasure. He had intended to make love to her. His body had been as eager as her own. But at the very last minute some mental barrier had triumphed and he had drawn back.

Damiano reappeared, a towel knotted round lean hips. 'I'm sorry,' he breathed starkly. 'I thought I could be cool about it...but I can't be. I can't make love to you with this much anger in me. I might have hurt you.'

He said all that without looking at her once as if the very sight of her was suddenly an offence to him. His bronzed profile fiercely taut, he went through to the connecting dressing room where she heard him slamming through units and drawers and then talking on the phone in Italian. She just sat there white-faced and sick inside. Damiano might as well have hung out a placard printed with the words. 'The end'. It was eleven at night. He had got out of bed, he was getting dressed.

She stood up, walked over to the open door and eavesdropped as he spoke tersely on the phone. Then she went into retreat again because she knew she was out of her depth and currently at a stand. She had told the truth and he could not accept it. He had contrived, however, to put on the act of the century. He had kept his rage under wraps. He was, she registered on a flood of desperate love, in infinitely more turmoil than she was.

He emerged from the dressing room, sheathed in a formal dark suit, hard, dark face as remote as the Andes. 'I'm going back to London—'

'Let me come with you...*please*.'

'I need some time,' Damiano breathed harshly, lifting a lean hand that wasn't quite steady in an expressive motion that he did not complete. 'You don't want to be around me right now. I need to be on my own.'

'Like Greta Garbo...' she muttered helplessly.

'*Accidenti!* You think I'm running away from this?' Damiano roared at her, his control splintering into black fury right in front of her. She fell back a step in sheer fright. 'I'm leaving for *your* sake. If I stay, I will very probably destroy what we have and I don't want to do that, so give me some space.'

Dully she nodded and turned her pained eyes away. 'I love you—'

'It doesn't feel like it,' Damiano ground out, his accent very thick.

The most dreadful silence set in.

'I've bought another country house in England...it was supposed to be a surprise,' Damiano admitted bleakly. 'You can go there as soon as you like. I'll make the arrangements.'

'You're going back to the town house to live,' she assumed, feeling as if she had been kicked. It was a separation, whatever he chose to call it.

'No. The bank has an apartment I can use.'

Long after Damiano had gone, Eden sat on in the empty bedroom. She felt gutted. Was this the end of the transition period that she had been warned about?

Stop avoiding the real issue here, her conscience urged her. Almost five years ago, she had created the current situation by being weak, sentimental and foolish. Damiano had come through hell to come home. No matter what the risk, it would have been wiser to tell him the whole story immediately. Secrecy and evasion did not instil trust. She, who had once prided herself on her honesty and her scruples, was ashamed of her own behaviour in retrospect. In *his* position, she too would have been angry, bitter and suspicious.

Forty-eight hours after Damiano's departure, Eden flew back to London and was driven out to Greyscott Hall.

It was a charming Elizabethan manor house set in wooded parkland. Damiano had phoned her twice since his return to London but the smooth impersonality of those dialogues had done little to raise her spirits. Indeed as she walked into the beautiful hall scented with the sweet perfume of a gorgeous arrangement of roses she was anxiously thinking that Damiano had cunningly contrived to rehouse her. Should he decide not to return to their marriage, he would not have the inconvenience of either moving himself or asking her to move.

'The instant I saw the video tape the agent sent, I knew you'd fall in love with Greyscott,' Damiano had informed her expressionlessly on the phone. 'It's full of character. It's big but it's not pretentious. It has a homely aspect.'

To Eden's knowledge, no Braganzi, raised from birth to consider magnificence their natural milieu, had ever aspired to live in any building which might be described by that word, 'homely.' Was it any wonder that she should feel nervous when Damiano had emphasised that Greyscott Hall was to be the home of *her* dreams?

The housekeeper took Eden on a guided tour. Even in the troubled mood she was in, Eden was entranced by her surroundings. Knole sofas covered with tapestry and a delightful window-seat adorned the sunlit room which overlooked the rose garden. Damiano had bought some of the contents of the house. He had also hired a design company to furnish the empty spaces in the main reception rooms and the master bedroom, so that the hall was ready for immediate occupation. So far, Eden had not been able to tell what was original and what was not and she was impressed by the care that had been taken. That timeless air of welcoming warmth and ever so slightly faded charm which was the hallmark of an old country house had been maintained.

'I believe you're a keen needlewoman,' the house-keeper remarked with a warm smile, spreading wide the door on a wonderful sewing room kitted out with every possible aid for such a purpose.

'Yes, I am.' But tears of disconcertion pricked Eden's eyes as she studied the array of equipment which included an elegant antique tapestry frame. Obviously Damiano remembered her stitching away all those years ago in the drawing room at the town house. In those days, she had used sewing as a distraction. With her hands busy and her head bent, it had been easier to ignore the snide comments and scornful looks which had come her way when Damiano had not been present.

Eden walked over to the window and kept her eyes very wide until she had herself under control again. The male who had gone to so much trouble on her behalf had really thought about what would make her happy. It was ironic that the evidence of Damiano's desire to surprise and please her should now inspire only a distressed awareness of what she had so recently lost.

Everything at Greyscott Hall had been planned and executed *before* Damiano had received that newspaper cutting.

Would she ever see Damiano again? She could not prove that she had remained faithful to their marriage. Nor in the circumstances did she feel that she could fault his distrust. As she wandered round the upper floor of her new home, it seemed perfectly credible to her that Damiano might not physically meet with her again. It would be so much easier for him to write their marriage off and call in the lawyers. After all, he had managed to live without her for a very long time. Surely he would remind himself of that unfortunate reality?

How much had those ecstatically happy weeks at the Villa Pavone actually *meant* to Damiano? Wasn't she inclined to place far too much importance on what they had shared? In fact, wasn't she guilty of being hopelessly naive? Damiano had spent four and a half years in prison. Then he had flown to Italy to embark on sun-filled weeks of sexual intimacy with a very willing and available partner and all the freedom, relaxation and comfort he could handle. Just about *any* man, fresh from a similar ordeal, would have thoroughly revelled in all that was on offer!

Hurriedly suppressing thoughts which threatened to drag her down into despair, Eden stilled the doorway of a room whose former purpose was still evident in the built-in corner cupboard. The worn hand-painted panels depicted children's toys. The nursery, she reflected gloomily—the nursery destined *never* to be filled.

But mere seconds in the wake of that thought, an extraordinary realisation struck Eden. Naturally, she was no longer taking the contraceptive pill which she has used when they had first been married. Well, whoopee, Eden, why has it taken until now for you to recall that fact? Dumbstruck by the belated awareness that she and Damiano had been making love without the slightest consideration of consequences for several weeks, Eden walked very slowly downstairs to be served with morning tea.

Damiano's miraculous return from the dead had simply blasted all such practicalities from her mind, Eden acknowledged in a daze. It had been almost five years since either of them had been required to consider precautions against pregnancy. Well…Damiano had not been any quicker off the mark than she had been on that count. Indeed, babies might well have come via the stork story the way the two of them had been behaving!

Eden almost knocked her cup and saucer over as she made a sudden lunge at her bag to dig out her diary. Another wave of that irritating dizziness washed over her, forcing her to lift her head again and breathe in deep before she felt able to check dates in her diary. She thought about the light-headed sensations which had been annoying her for almost a week and discovered that her period was a few days late. Her cycle was normally regular.

A beatific glow slowly enveloped Eden. She might be pregnant right now, she thought in shock; right this very minute, she might be pregnant! And how would Damiano feel about that? Well, the guy who had said he was tough would just have to *be* tough. What she really needed was confirmation one way or the other from a doctor and she wasted no time in reaching for the phone.

After Damiano had gone missing, Eden had just about broken her heart over that reality that there had not been the slightest chance of her being pregnant.

Although she had chosen to stop taking the contraceptive pill, Damiano had not shared her bed again in those final weeks. She had believed then that in her situation a child would have been an enormous comfort.

As soon as she had had lunch, Eden was driven back to London to keep an immediate appointment with the Harley Street medical practitioner whom the Braganzi family patronised. She prayed while the pregnancy test was being done. Twenty minutes later, she settled back into the limo shaken, smug and over the moon.

Indeed, Eden did not begin descending to planet earth again until she went to bed that night in solitary state at Greyscott Hall. With increasing anxiety, she was by then wondering how Damiano would react to the news that she was carrying his child. The insane desire to rush straight to the phone and tell him in the hope of bringing him home had receded fast. Five years ago, admitting to Damiano that she wanted a baby had gone down like a lead balloon. And how could Damiano possibly want her to have his baby now when they were estranged?

Everything always seemed to condense down to one humiliating fact: Damiano did not love her. If he had ever loved her, he would have told her. She had never forgotten Annabel Stavely, egged on by Cosetta, showing off her necklace etched with a loving inscription from Damiano. Even so, back then, she had often wondered what Damiano had found *to* love in Annabel. The redhead's undeniable physical perfection? Her endless joy in shopping? Her enthusiastic description of each designer garment purchased? Her apparent inability to utter a single intelligent sentence? While prepared to admit that she had scarcely been an unprejudiced judge, Eden had been stumped.

At noon the next day, having entertained herself with a trip to the nearest design and interiors shop and returned with a couple of wallpaper books, Eden was down on her knees in the nursery. To cheer herself up, she was comparing the merits of fluffy bunny rabbits on a border as opposed to dancing teddy bears, and when she heard footsteps behind her she simply assumed it was the housekeeper.

'What do you think?' she asked.

'Love those drunk-looking teddy bears...' Damiano breathed without warning above her head. 'But why are the rabbits jumping over gates like sheep?'

Eden froze.

'Artistic licence, I expect,' Damiano answered for himself, his dark, deep drawl so constrained it screamed his tension louder than any tannoy. 'Not very sophisticated but certainly novel.'

CHAPTER NINE

IN DISCOMFITED haste, Eden flipped shut both the wallpaper books. 'I wasn't expecting you,' she admitted before she could think better of it.

'Do I need to make an appointment now?' Damiano enquired tautly.

'Of course not.' Eden did not notice the hand he extended to help her up off her knees. She was flustered and waiting for him to ask why she had been studying nursery wallpapers. She smoothed down her fitted short-sleeved apricot blouse and the toning cotton skirt she wore with nervous hands. 'When did you arrive?'

Damiano flashed her a narrowed glance from spectacular dark, deep-set eyes, high cheekbones taut. 'Almost an hour ago. I expected to stumble upon you faster.'

He had been in no hurry to find her, Eden translated, heart sinking at that amount of reluctance after a separation which had lasted three days. Not that three days was that long a space of time, she tried to tell herself. She focused on him with helpless intensity, greedily absorbing every detail of his appearance. The sophisticated pale grey suit cut to enhance every hard line of his wide shoulders, narrow hips and long, powerful thighs. The black silk luxuriance of hair, the strong masculine profile, the authority and intrinsic sensuality of a breathtakingly attractive and powerful male.

'To be frank, I was thinking…thinking in depth,' Damiano extended flatly, snapping her out of the ab-

158

stracted thoughts that were already beginning to make
her face burn. 'Trying to work out what to say to you
and, I'm afraid, not getting anywhere fast.'

That honest admission struck Eden with force and
filled her with fear. Nobody with any finer feeling found
it easy to find the right words with which to break news
that would hurt. 'Let's go downstairs,' she urged,
swiftly stepping past him.

No, he wasn't the type to bring in the lawyers without
telling her first face to face that he wanted a divorce.
There was nothing cowardly about Damiano and nothing underhand. His cool reserve might once have defied
her comprehension but he had returned to her, consid-
erably more willing to express what he felt and what he
thought. Her fingers fluttered across her tummy in a
fleeting protective gesture that she hurriedly cut short.
Telling Damiano that she was expecting their first child
promised to be a most humiliating challenge. From his
point of view, that could hardly be good news, but she
had no doubt that he would politely strive to hide that
reality for her sake. Her throat thickened with tears.

Damiano followed Eden into the sitting room. Eden
left him again to order coffee but she was ashamed of
that weak prompting to play for time. The arrival of
coffee was hardly likely to deflect Damiano from his
purpose.

When she reappeared, Damiano was lodged by the
stone fireplace. The angles of his lean, strong face were
tense. 'It's ironic to think that this is really our first
home. I don't think the town house counts.'

Eden was at the stage of reading threatening vibra-
tions into everything that now passed his lips. She was
convinced that the irony he saw in his purchase of
Greyscott Hall as their first supposed home was that he

now knew he would never *share* it with her. 'No, I suppose it doesn't,' she agreed tightly. 'Are you planning to sell the Villa Pavone?'

Dark golden eyes veiled, Damiano shot her a sudden frowning glance. 'That idea hadn't occurred to me. But I believe that the villa should be opened to the public for some part of the year in honour of my grandmother's work.'

A light knock on the door heralded the arrival of coffee. Eden busied herself over the cups but her hands were all fingers and thumbs and she had to do everything very slowly. The atmosphere was so full of charged undertones that her tummy was in knots and her palms damp.

'*Grazie…*' Damiano breathed flatly, retreating back to the fireplace with his cup and saucer as if there were a dividing line down the centre of the room and he could only briefly visit the zone designated as hers. 'Do you like the house?'

'It's really beautiful. I was delighted with the sewing room too. That was a lovely idea,' Eden completed in a voice that just trailed away on the reflection that that reminder of his warmer intentions towards her might now be unwelcome.

Across the room, a shaft of sunlight playing over his dark, well-shaped head, Damiano stared down fixedly into his black coffee.

Eden feasted her attention on him, noting the taut line of his beautifully shaped mouth, and then watched his cup rattle on the saucer for a split second before she realised that he couldn't hold his hand quite steady. Almost as quickly, Damiano set his coffee down with a low-pitched exclamation in Italian.

Strained dark eyes claimed hers before she could

evade that contact. 'I very much regret what happened in Italy—'

Eden went rigid, registering that the main issue could no longer be avoided. 'Fine, absolutely fine,' she slotted in with a mindless desire to stop him speaking before he could say anything that might hurt her.

The silence smouldered.

'No, it *wasn't* fine,' Damiano contradicted. 'I should never have reacted as I did. I owe you an explanation.'

Eden tore her pained gaze from his. She rose from her seat because sitting still had suddenly become impossible for her and she walked over to the windows. She did not want any long-winded explanations. She *knew* how he felt; she wasn't stupid. He had been willing to give their marriage another chance but the belief that she had had an affair had blown that ambition out of the water.

'When I saw that newspaper cutting, I was confronted by my biggest fear,' Damiano admitted in a driven undertone. 'And I am very conscious that I did not shine like a star in dealing with it.'

'But I understood how you felt,' Eden conceded heavily.

That tabloid story furnished with a convincing photograph and backed by her own suspicious silence on the subject would not have impressed any man with a belief in her innocence.

'I doubt it...'

Eden looked up uncertainly.

Damiano studied her with bleak dark eyes. 'I thought the worst because I felt that I *deserved* the worst. I was too upset to be rational,' he confessed with a ragged edge to his dark, deep drawl. 'But even when I was being a lousy husband five years ago, even when I was

being unreasonably jealous, I always knew in my heart
that you were the most honest and sincere woman I had
ever met.'

'You…you did?' Eden pressed in surprise.

'*Of course*, I did,' Damiano asserted forcefully. 'No
matter how damning the evidence appeared, I should
have accepted your word that you had not had an affair
with Mark Anstey.'

Eden continued to stare at him, utterly disconcerted
by that final statement. Meeting the level look of regret
in his spectacular dark golden eyes, she realised that he
meant what he was saying. No longer did he suspect
that she had been unfaithful! The most enormous tide
of relief rolled over Eden and left her feeling weak. She
sank heavily down on the window-seat and slowly
breathed in deep to steady herself.

'I wish I could tell you that I reached that conclusion
without hesitation,' Damiano continued with a pronounced air of discomfiture. 'But I'm afraid I can't—'

'You can't?' Eden cut in anxiously, wondering if she
had misunderstood his declaration of faith in her mere
seconds earlier.

'I was able to purchase the entire roll of film that was
taken of Anstey and his female companion that day.'
Damiano withdrew several photographs from the inside
pocket of his jacket. Colour scored his hard cheekbones
as Eden frowned in bewilderment and then stared
fixedly down at the snaps he was laying out on the
window-seat for her inspection.

'I didn't realise that there was more than that one
photograph taken!' Eden snatched up the first. She was
astonished to find herself studying a photo of Tina in
the act of climbing out of the car, a photo which nobody

who knew both women could possibly have mistaken as being of Eden.

'I had begun negotiations to buy that film before I even landed back in London,' Damiano informed her wryly. 'I wanted to ensure that neither the original nor any further photos that might have been taken that day could appear in print again.'

Eden slowly shook her head over the spread. Distaste filled her as she thought of the hidden photographer out simply for profit but ultimately responsible for causing so much heartache. Leaving the photos where they lay, she got up and walked away from them in growing disgust and bitterness. 'Naturally, the newspaper was only interested in printing that one picture that showed the big kiss but not the woman's face! So it was just a case of mistaken identity, was it? Some creep who didn't know either Tina or me well enough to tell us apart?'

'I have put the matter in the hands of my lawyers. My opinion is that the mistake was deliberate because it provided a tacky little story but I may be proved wrong. Can you forgive me for doubting you?' Damiano demanded tautly.

'Oh, don't be stupid!' Eden exclaimed, still outraged by what she had learnt from seeing those photographs. 'I'm just so annoyed that I didn't have the wit to get in touch with the family legal firm and order my own investigation years ago!'

Crossing the room, Damiano reached for her tightly clenched hands. He closed his fingers over hers. 'Eden…?' he prompted grittily. 'I'll beg if you want me to.'

Her hands relaxed in the grip of his. She forgot all about the photographs as finally she allowed herself to fully appreciate that the nightmare was over. Happiness

began to surge up where once there had only been fear
and anxiety. She looked up at him and collided with
shimmering eyes that made her heart sing. 'Would you
beg?' she could not resist asking with considerable curiosity.

'*Per amour di Dio*...' Damiano murmured with ragged stress, almost crushing the life from her smaller
hands. 'Could you doubt it after what we were to each
other in Italy, *tesora mio*? Don't you know that even if
it *had* been you in that photo, I would have come back
to you?'

'Really?' Eden gazed up at him with shaken eyes.

'Now you're being stupid...' Damiano muttered with
roughened tenderness, gathering her into his arms and
releasing his breath in a pent-up hiss. 'I only came back
to London because I was afraid of wrecking what we
had found together.'

'An excess of tact doesn't become you...or suit me.
I would have preferred you to stay and talk,' Eden confided, her mouth running dry and the breath shortening
in her throat.

Being pressed into intimate connection with his lithe,
powerful physique awakened little quivers of responsive
heat in what felt like every inch of her body. A very
feminine smile curved her lips as he shivered against
her, his heated male arousal something he could not
conceal from her.

'*Sì*...' Turning up her face, Damiano appraised her
with scorching golden eyes and then, linking his hands
with hers again, he groaned unevenly. 'I have missed
being with you so much. Could we complete this conversation upstairs, *cara mia*?'

Eden pretended to consider his request and tilted her
head to one side. Her eyes danced with provocation.

With a censorious growl, Damiano responded by sealing his hot demanding mouth to hers. Soaring excitement laced her haze of joyous happiness. He released her long enough for them to reach the hall and start up the stairs, but a couple of minutes were lost on the landing when the temptation to kiss again proved too much for both of them.

Damiano deposited her on the bed in the dark oak-panelled master bedroom. Eden kicked off her shoes. 'Can't you just imagine this room lit by fire-light in winter?' she whispered, studying him with dreamy eyes, clasping her hands over her still flat tummy and deciding that she would tell him about the baby after they had made love.

Damiano gave her a slanting grin. 'I like you in all kinds of light. I'm not at all particular in that direction.'

Her heart just jumped at the innate charm of that smile.

'Daylight, moonlight, lamplight, total blackout...' Damiano enumerated in mocking addition, tugging loose his silk tie and removing his jacket with a decided look of intent that made her tense with anticipation. 'I can't believe you're not throwing me out—'

Eden lifted a slim shoulder in an attempt to emulate one of his slight fluid shrugs. 'I could still be considering it—'

Still half dressed, Damiano came down on the bed and cupped her cheekbones with his spread fingers. 'Don't tease,' he urged feelingly, lustrous dark eyes pinned to her tender smile in raw approach. 'I have no sense of humour whatsoever when it comes to the idea of losing you.'

She turned her lips into his hand and kissed his palm. 'That cuts both ways,' she said a little shakily.

Their eyes met, hot gold into anxious green, and suddenly they were kissing each other breathless with the kind of electrifying mutual hunger which brooked no denial. Eden wrenched at his shirt buttons at the same time as he attempted to deprive her of her blouse. With a groan of frustration at their colliding manoeuvres, Damiano pulled back and ripped off his shirt, sending a couple of buttons flying in his eagerness to discard it.

'Not very cool, Mr Braganzi—'

'Not feeling cool at all,' Damiano confided without hesitation, extracting her from her blouse and disposing of her bra.

He pressed his mouth hotly to the exposed slope of one small breast, succumbed to the lure of a pouting pink nipple and lingered there to tease her sensitive flesh with erotic mastery. She writhed under his attentions, possessed by a frantic craving that drove her on like a fever. He ran his hand up the extended length of one slender thigh, driving her wild with anticipation. She closed her hand into his hair, dragging his mouth back to hers again, straining up to him as his tongue delved hungrily into the tender interior of her mouth, leaving her quivering helplessly in reaction.

'I can't wait to be inside you, *cara*,' Damiano swore raggedly as he pushed up her skirt and deftly removed her panties.

'Don't wait...' Her every nerve-ending felt tightly stretched. She was so hot, so excited, she couldn't keep still. Her own impatience was unbearable. She wanted him; she wanted him *now*.

Damiano studied her with smouldering eyes of desire. She rocked up against him and his brilliant eyes suddenly flared stormy gold. He pulled her under him and sank into her with one bold, hungry thrust. For an instant she was shocked by the sheer surge of wanton pleasure. And then her hunger for him took her over again, wild and uncontrollable and torturously sweet as the lithe male dominance of his body over, and in, hers. Her heart was racing as he drove her higher and higher, her whole being centred on reaching that ultimate plateau. The explosion of ecstatic pleasure splintered through her with unforgettable strength and then dropped her slowly again back into the hold of her body.

In the aftermath, she held him close, awash with wonder and a little shock and loving tenderness. Damiano smoothed her hair, dropped a kiss on her brow, rolled back, but he kept her securely pinned to him with a possessiveness more than equal to her own.

'It's so special with you...' Damiano murmured with slumbrous satisfaction.

Her lips curved. 'And yet you said that what happened in the bedroom wasn't important enough to make a major issue,' she reminded him.

Damiano lifted her up to look at her. His brilliant eyes were full of devilment. 'Step one in my seduction plan was to defuse the tension—'

'Seduction plan?'

'I thought it would take weeks and weeks for us to make it this far,' Damiano confided with rueful amusement.

They lay in a relaxed sprawl. Damiano hugged her close and drawled. 'I've dealt with Anstey, by the way—'

'Mark?'

Damiano smiled like a sleepy tiger, eyes gleaming below dark lashes. 'He won't be bothering you again—'

'What happened?' she pressed anxiously.

Damiano shifted a noncommittal shoulder. 'He's repaid the money and he'll think twice before he tries blackmail a second time.'

Eden sat up. '*Damiano…*'

'I hit him. OK?' Damiano gave her a level look of challenge. 'He frightened you. He caused you a lot of distress. He's lucky I didn't damage him permanently!'

Eden never approved of violence. Her principles fought with her lack of sympathy for Mark, whose callous behaviour had hurt her a great deal. While she was struggling with those opposing feelings, the phone by the bed rang.

Damiano reached for the receiver. His lean, strong face tensed, expressive mouth tightening. 'We'll be down in ten minutes.'

'Who is it?'

'Nuncio and Cosetta are here,' Damiano breathed, springing off the bed and a grim look in his eyes. 'I should never have given Nuncio the name of this place and I should have made time for him this morning when he phoned asking to see me, but I'm afraid I wasn't in the mood for my little brother.'

'You can't tell Nuncio about Tina's affair,' Eden warned him flatly.

'That's not your decision to make,' Damiano retorted with crisp clarity. 'You might have been prepared to let yourself be hung out to dry on Tina's behalf, but I'm not. In any case, my family was abusing you *long* before that tabloid story appeared!'

'But you don't repay spite with spite—'

'No, you repay wrong with right,' Damiano countered, unmoved by that line or argument. 'I won't listen to a single word spoken against you, so, for his own

sake, I hope Nuncio has not come here with the intent
of causing trouble.'

They went downstairs together. Eden was dismayed
when she walked into the sitting room and registered
that Damiano's entire family had chosen to descend on
them. Nuncio, Cosetta and Tina were seated round the
fireplace. But she almost laughed when she heard
Damiano stifle a groan of exasperation at the same sight.

CHAPTER TEN

NUNCIO looked deeply uncomfortable, like a man who had been dragged somewhere he didn't want to be by the women in his life. His sister, Cosetta, gave him a charged look of expectancy and, when he failed to react, she rose to her feet with a pronounced air of self-importance.

'We need to talk to you in private, Damiano.'

Damiano dealt the sharp-faced brunette a withering appraisal. 'Eden's my wife and she stays, Cosetta.'

'I think Eden and I should go for a walk.' Tina stood up with one of her little deprecating smiles. 'What do you say, Eden? Shall we leave the Braganzis to it?'

'Not just right now, thanks,' Eden said quietly.

China-blue eyes hardening, Tina sat down again.

Nuncio began to say something in Italian to his brother.

'Let's stick to English,' Damiano cut in.

'I'll find this matter very difficult to broach with Eden present,' Nuncio protested.

'Then you have a problem because I'm not going anywhere,' Eden advised her brother-in-law, disconcerting him with a sharp retort such as he had never received from her before. But then Eden had already decided that the days when she had allowed Damiano's siblings to snub and embarrass her were long behind her.

'Oh, for goodness' sake,' Cosetta exclaimed, throwing Nuncio a look of stark impatience. 'This secrecy

170

has gone on long enough. Annabel's being very silly keeping herself in the background but we're supposed to be here to put things right for her!'

Eden blinked in surprise at that reference to Damiano's former fiancée. Why on earth was Damiano's sister rabbiting on about Annabel Stavely?

'What are you trying to put right for Annabel?' Eden enquired but even Cosetta, who was normally a far from sensitive being, coloured and looked away from her, sooner than answer her directly.

'We wanted Annabel to come out to Brazil with us…Annabel and her son, Peter,' Nuncio began stiffly, his heavy face flushed as he concentrated his attention on his elder brother. 'But she became quite hysterical when we suggested that—'

'Of course, she did. She has her pride. Naturally she didn't want to be the one to make the first move. Any woman would feel the same in her position!' Cosetta proclaimed in heated defence of her best friend.

Eden slowly shook her head in silent wonderment. Damiano's family never failed to astonish her. Not only had they left her behind when they had flown out to greet their long-lost brother in Brazil, but they had also evidently attempted to persuade Annabel to take what should have been Eden's place! As for Cosetta's fond contention that Annabel was too proud to make the first move with Damiano…well, Eden almost laughed out loud at that claim. In her efforts to win Damiano back even after his marriage, Annabel had been blatant.

Admittedly, it had never seemed to get the redhead anywhere, Eden conceded. She might have envied Annabel because she believed that Damiano had once sincerely loved the other woman. But even thinking that Damiano might well have married her on the rebound,

Eden had recognised that he'd no longer been in love with his former fiancée. Indeed, had she had a better sense of humour five years earlier, she might well have reaped a lot of macabre enjoyment from Annabel's attempts to attract Damiano when he'd been so patently detached from her.

'What is this farrago of nonsense?' Damiano enquired very drily of his brother and sister. 'Why would you have invited Annabel to come out to Brazil with you? Why the hell would I have wanted to see her?'

'So that you could be tempted afresh,' Eden could not resist pointing out to her husband, a slight wobble in her voice. 'Your family obviously thought it was too good an opportunity to miss. After all, you had spent all those years locked up and were sure to be at a low ebb of restraint!'

An appreciative smile curved Damiano's mouth and he closed his arm round Eden. 'Why do you think that I'm still complaining that *you* weren't on the flight?' he teased before turning his attention back to his brother. 'Come on, Nuncio. Do try to come to the point.'

Nuncio cleared his throat like a bullfrog and stood up. 'Annabel has had a child, Damiano...'

Eden's spine tingled and stiffened. Only now did she recall Tina smugly telling her that she had a huge shock coming her way. Common sense told her what had to be coming next but she just couldn't credit the explanation that her mind was serving up to her.

'*So?*' Damiano elevated a sardonic dark brow.

'Annabel told us that you and she had got back together again shortly before you went out to Montavia,' Cosetta delivered and the brunette slung a triumphant smile at Eden's astonished face. 'We weren't at all surprised but poor Annabel didn't feel she could tell us the truth until your wife had moved out of the town house. By then Annabel was five months pregnant and, with her father having been declared bankrupt, she was very much in need of our support—'

'Annabel will be in even greater need of your support when she finds herself hauled up in court for slander,' Damiano broke in with icy disbelief, his outrage etched in every angle of hard bone-structure. 'How *dare* you bring this tissue of lies into my home? If Annabel has had a child, it was *not* fathered by me!'

Eden had gone way beyond amusement now. She felt sick with shock. And she thought strickenly for an instant, *Could* it be true? Might Damiano have turned to Annabel again before he'd gone missing and when their marriage had been under strain? She looked up at him and found him gazing down intently at her. She met his eyes head on, those stunning clear dark golden eyes. She recognised the honest anger there, the pure exasperation with which one met a fantastic story, and not the smallest shade of discomfiture. Her momentary stab of concern vanished to be replaced with outrage. It was his wretched family again, she decided furiously, still set on having another go at dividing them!

'That's quite some story, Cosetta,' Eden commented tightly, her green eyes sparkling with scorn. 'Very offensive in its content but just a little too like a soap opera to impress anyone with any wit!'

'Annabel *said* that Peter was Damiano's son!' Cosetta argued shrilly.

In the face of his elder brother's outraged rebuttal, Nuncio had turned a pasty colour and fallen silent. Now he said uneasily, 'Ever since Damiano came home, Annabel has done nothing but beg us to mind our own business and keep quiet about this, Cosetta. I told you

I wasn't happy with the odd way she's been behaving—'

'That's only because Annabel wanted Damiano to make a free choice between her and Eden,' Cosetta argued even more frantically. 'Annabel *wouldn't* have lied to me!'

'What you seem to forget is that your brother made that choice when he married me,' Eden retorted with crisp dismissal. 'It's long past time that his family accepted that and, if you can't accept it, then leave us alone.'

'I couldn't have put it better myself,' Damiano stated flatly, curving Eden even closer to his big powerful frame as he surveyed their three visitors. 'And, sadly, you, my family, really *do* deserve Annabel. Indeed Annabel could not have ripped off a nicer set of people. I can barely believe how stupid you've all been—'

'Ripped off? Stupid?' Cosetta repeated incredulously. 'How can you say that?'

'Annabel waits until she thinks I'm dead and Eden has been driven from the family before she comes forward with her touching little confession…am I right?' Damiano prompted, sounding very bored.

'Well…yes,' Nuncio confirmed.

'She then told you she was expecting my child. Tell me, did anybody argue at that point? Did anybody seek any supporting evidence of her claim?' Damiano surveyed his siblings with questioning derision. 'So you just accepted that if Annabel was pregnant, the child was mine because she *said* so. Even though I was married—'

'Annabel said you were planning on getting a divorce.' Nuncio groaned.

'*Annabel said,*' Damiano stressed with angry contempt. 'Her father going bankrupt must've been a really nasty shock because Annabel has expensive tastes. Weren't you capable of adding two and two and making four, Nuncio? Didn't you smell the proverbial rat? How much money have you given her over the years?'

'I can't believe that Annabel could have made it all up just to get money off us! How could she *do* that to me?' Cosetta sobbed and she stalked over to the window and turned her back on them all.

'You used her to get at me, Cosetta,' Eden reminded the brunette ruefully. 'And she used you to stay in Damiano's radius.'

'Ouch...' Damiano groaned.

Looking hangdog, Nuncio muttered defensively, 'I was only trying to look out for *your* interests when I helped Annabel out, Damiano—'

'How? By hurting and humiliating my wife when she was at her most vulnerable? Tell me, how was *that* looking out for my interests?' Damiano demanded with a hard condemnation that made his younger brother flinch.

China-blue eyes cold as charity, Tina now spoke up with her usual hesitancy. 'I'm sorry but it's really not fair to blame Nuncio,' she said softly. 'None of us have wanted to mention it but Eden *did* have an affair with another man and obviously that upset all of us a great deal.'

Bitter anger flared in Eden at Tina's nerve in making that crack. She felt electric aggression power tension through every muscle in Damiano's lean, well-built length. 'Tina...' Damiano began not quite evenly, rage gritting from even those two single syllables, but he did not get the chance to continue.

Without the smallest warning, Cosetta erupted back

into the centre of the room and pitched a set of prints down onto Tina's lap. 'You lying, cheating little snake!' she spat furiously. 'It was *you* who had the affair with Mark Anstey! It was you all along and you lied all the way down the line!'

As Eden fixed appalled eyes on the photos she now belatedly recalled having left lying on the window-seat, close to where Cosetta had been standing, all hell broke loose. Nuncio made a sudden grab at the photographs and broke into an aghast exclamation while Cosetta continued her ranting attack on her former ally.

'You can stage this confrontation elsewhere,' Damiano drawled with chilling clarity. Striding over to the door, he flung it wide. 'All of you...*out*!'

Shattered silence fell.

'I'm prepared to get physical,' Damiano warned.

Their unwelcome visitors departed but they were all shouting at each other again before the front door even closed behind them. Eden sagged with relief.

'They will never set foot in any residence of ours again,' Damiano swore with vehemence. 'But when did my kid sister turn into such a shrew?'

Eden sighed and, turning round, rested her brow against his broad chest, feeling his arms close round her and revelling in the warmth and solidity of him. 'I think her friendship with Annabel turned her in that direction. Annabel is a lot older and she influenced her a good deal. Oh, dear...I feel so awful about leaving those dreadful photos just sitting there where anyone could find them!'

'I noticed them long before Cosetta did. I was subconsciously *willing* Nuncio to go over there and see them, *cara mia*,' Damiano confided grimly, strongly disconcerting her. 'Tina has not been good company for Cosetta either—'

'But what about Nuncio? He looked so stricken, Damiano—'

'He's miserable with her or hadn't you noticed that yet? Let them work out their own problems,' Damiano advised. 'I don't have any sympathy to spare after that outrageous spiel about Annabel. Listening to them, I honestly wondered if my brother and sister had more than one brain cell apiece—'

'But you'll note that I had *total* faith in you,' Eden informed him with the kind of sweetness that carried a slight sting in its tail.

Dark colour accentuated his blunt cheekbones just as a knock sounded on the door and it opened. Their housekeeper began to speak but was silenced by the woman pushing impatiently past her to gain entrance to the room.

It was Annabel Stavely and Annabel as Eden had never seen her before. The redhead had no make-up on, swollen eyes and a look of desperation etched on her still beautiful face.

'You've got to let me explain myself!' Annabel exclaimed pleadingly.

'Do you think you could make it brief?' Damiano enquired very drily.

'I passed the limo at the end of the driveway,' Annabel confided in a rush and bit at her full lower lip. 'I hoped I'd get here first so that I could explain but I know that Nuncio and Cosetta must already have told you about the story I made up—'

'Children make up stories. Adults tell lies.' Damiano shot Annabel a derisive appraisal. 'And when an adult lies to commit a fraud, it is rather more serious. So let's not pretend that you involved yourself in some playful little charade—'

Annabel was very pale. 'I didn't see that it was going to hurt anybody—'

'You didn't *care* whether it did or not,' Eden cut in helplessly. 'For you to have pretended that your child was my husband's is about as low as any woman could sink—'

'How many other people are suffering from the same delusion?' Damiano demanded with sudden harshness, that aspect clearly not having occurred to him until Eden mentioned it.

'Only your family,' Annabel hastened to assure him. 'It really was a big secret—'

'It had better have been or you will find yourself in court,' Damiano spelt out in hard warning. 'If one rumour of this appears in print, call your solicitor because you're going to need him.'

Annabel surveyed him with appalled eyes and then dropped her head.

'Does your son believe that Damiano is his father?' Eden had to ask.

'No! Really, you're making far too much of this,' Annabel contended shakily. 'It was wrong and it was stupid but I was so broke I couldn't even settle the rent on my apartment! Don't you realise the *hell* I've gone through this last month since Damiano turned up alive?'

At that plea for sympathy on such a count, Eden's lips parted company and then sealed together again for she dared not have spoken.

'I mean I just couldn't *believe* you coming back from the dead like that!' Annabel wailed accusingly at Damiano. 'Do you think I'd have lied if I'd known there was any chance of that happening? I had to take myself off to a friend's villa in Turkey to hide. I didn't know what I was going to do to get myself out of this mess. And Cosetta kept on phoning and phoning and *phoning* me to demand that I fly out to Italy to see you! You were the very *last* person I wanted to see!'

'You've had a really dreadful time,' Eden muttered soothingly but she was challenged to keep her face straight.

Damiano murmured tautly, 'I don't think we need to discuss this any further, Annabel—'

'You mean you forgive me?'

Damiano sighed. 'Annabel…unless I've very much mistaken you have managed to defraud my brother of thousands of pounds over the last few years. You ripped him off and what *he* chooses to do about that is nothing to do with me.'

Apparently shaken by the realisation that she could not magically solve her every problem by begging Damiano to forgive her, Annabel departed with a lot less drama than she had arrived.

'We're out,' Damiano then instructed their house-keeper. 'I don't care who comes to the door. We're not here.'

Eden was feeling incredibly sleepy. Damiano took one look at her wan face and drooping head and he scooped her off her seat and carried her back upstairs. 'This has all been too much for you, *cara*—'

'Actually I'm so grateful I didn't miss out on hearing what an unwelcome shock you gave Annabel with your return from the dead!' Eden laughed helplessly at that recollection. 'I didn't *dare* look at you in case I went off into whoops. Are you finally going to tell me why you broke off your engagement to her?'

Damiano winced. 'Do I have to?'

'You *owe* me,' Eden told him playfully.

'I overheard a conversation she had with her sister. Her sister had just got engaged and she asked Annabel what she liked *most* about me,' Damiano related with a pained smile. 'And there was this huge silence and then Annabel finally said, "he's loaded and he's great in bed." That is the moment when the rot first set in.'

'She was probably joking—'

'Having had the pleasure of hearing that opinion, I naturally began paying closer attention to our relationship. I then found out that she wasn't at all averse to slipping into other men's beds when I was abroad,' Damiano shared wryly as he laid her down on the bed.

'Oh...' Eden rubbed her cheek against his shoulder, understanding why he had had no desire to tell her that particular tale before.

'I didn't tell my family why I'd ditched her. That *was* a mistake,' Damiano acknowledged. 'But I'd learned by then that my own feelings for Annabel were pretty shallow and I didn't care enough to disabuse them of their illusions.'

'Then you met me...' Eden was tiring of the subject of Annabel which had now been for ever shorn of further interest.

'That was love at first sight. Absolutely terrifying!' Damiano confided.

'Eden sat up with a start. 'Say that again—'

'Do I *have* to?' A charismatic smile curved Damiano's sensual mouth. 'Post-Annabel I was convinced that I was the coldest fish alive as far as women were concerned. I was very cynical and then I saw you and I swear that both my brain and my body went haywire the same second.'

'I don't believe I'm hearing this,' Eden framed in a daze.

Glittering dark eyes rested on her bemused face and he muttered ruefully, 'You're not going to like hearing the rest of it. In those days, I *hated* feeling like that and that added a certain hostility to our every encounter. I wanted to be in control...'

'And you thought you weren't in control because I wouldn't sleep with you,' Eden filled in for him with a sigh.

'No, there you're wrong, *amore*. As far as I was concerned, if you didn't want to make love with me, you couldn't possibly care about me or want me anything like as much as I cared about and wanted you.'

Even five years on, Eden was stricken by that revealing confession. She looked at him with reproachful eyes. 'Oh, *no*...'

'Oh, yes,' Damiano told her levelly. 'When I fell for you, love and sex were quite indivisible in my estimation. I'd never been in love in my life before but I couldn't believe you *could* love me and keep on freezing me out—'

Eden traced a regretful fingertip along his hard jawline. 'I had no idea that I could make you feel insecure back then. You always seemed so incredibly confident—'

Damiano caught her into his arms and held her fast, shimmering dark golden eyes scanning her with tender amusement. 'Call it like it was, *tesoro mio*,' he urged. 'I was arrogant and I just could not credit that a virgin could run rings round me—'

'I was very nervous of that kind of intimacy...but I think that if I'd known you loved me after we married, I would have felt very different,' Eden said slowly. 'Unfortunately, your sister told me about Annabel and then, when I came back from our honeymoon and finally *saw* Annabel, I thought that you most likely *had* married me on the rebound—'

'You and I were engaged for all of one week. I was engaged to her for two years and never got myself to the point of fixing a wedding date,' Damiano pointed out. 'I love you very, very much. Even when I was acting like a jerk, I never doubted that. I couldn't have handled it if I'd come home and you hadn't been here for me.'

Eden glowed with happiness. She rested her head down on his chest, listening to the slow, solid thump of his heart beating, drinking in the familiar scent of him. Then she smiled. 'How do you feel about having a baby?'

'On a scale of one to ten—ten being the height of keen,' Damiano informed her teasingly. 'Ten.'

'Sounds promising—'

Damiano vented a laugh. 'I have now finally reached the pinnacle of male maturity where I can consider a baby without being gripped by the devastating fear that you might feel *more* for the baby than you feel for me!'

'Even better. Are you aware that I haven't been on the contraceptive pill for years?'' Eden enquired, slowly raising her head to study him.

A slight frown-line drew his ebony brows together. 'I have to confess that I hadn't got around to thinking about technical stuff like that yet—'

'Technical stuff?' Eden queried chokily.

'When I'm in bed with you, I'm not exactly grounded...' Lustrous dark golden eyes suddenly settled on her with raw intensity. '*Accidenti!* If you're *not*...and *I* haven't been using—'

'You're going to be a father,' Eden told him softly.

Damiano rolled her gently flat against the pillows and stared fixedly down at her. 'Are you teasing me?'

'I'm pregnant,' Eden declared.

At that confirmation, Damiano hastily released her from a good half of his weight. 'That's fantastic!' he breathed, visibly stunned.

'But *not* breakable,' Eden added, hauling him back to her with possessive hands.

One year and one month later, Eden walked into the nursery at the Villa Pavone. Diamonds glittering at her wrist and in her ears, she was wearing a fabulous pale green ball gown in readiness for the big party they were throwing that evening.

Damiano was tucking in the twins. Their son, Niccolo, lay still like a little prince, big sleepy green eyes pinned to his father, but his twin sister, Chiara, was still wriggling. Damiano was endeavouring to mesmerise his infant daughter into more restful mode with the use of the musical mobile above the cot.

Eden smiled. She could still barely believe that she was the mother of two children. She had been a couple of months along before a scan had picked up the fact that she'd been carrying two babies, rather than just one. She had been delighted at the news but Damiano had been concerned that a twin pregnancy would be more risky. However, although Niccolo and Chiara had come into the world a little early as did most twins, both Eden and their children had come through fine.

The past year had been very eventful from start to finish. They had spent a lot of time in Italy, enjoying the rather more relaxed pace of their lifestyle there. Damiano had been re-elected Chairman of the Braganzi

Bank but he delegated much more, worked from home when he could and took her with him when he went abroad. Indeed, Eden had once or twice felt ever so slightly guilty that what had been a truly stupendous, wonderfully happy and successful year for her and Damiano had been something less for others.

Although there *had* been one light moment. Annabel Stavely had rushed off and married an elderly peer of the realm after Nuncio had informed her that he expected all the money he had given her repaid. Six months later, she had become a reasonably wealthy and, it had to be admitted, a fairly merry widow according to the gossip columns.

Then, just three months ago, Damiano had passed Eden a newspaper and had indicated a small article about Mark Anstey. Mark had been sent to prison for embezzling a huge amount of money from the unfortunate owners of the organic farm company. The biggest shock for Eden had been the discovery that that had *not* been Mark's first offence.

In the past year also, Nuncio and Tina had failed to mend their differences and had ended up going through a bitter divorce. During a heated quarrel, Tina had really lost her temper and had told Nuncio that their daughter, Allegra, was *not* his child. Nuncio had been devastated. Tina had then thought better of her honesty and had tried to persuade him that she had only been lying to hurt him. However, Nuncio had had DNA testing done and that had proved that Allegra could not be his. Even so, Nuncio had still insisted that he wanted to maintain contact with the little girl because he was very fond of her.

Damiano and Nuncio were now behaving like brothers again simply because Nuncio had become so depressed after that bombshell about Allegra that Damiano had had no choice but to offer sympathy and support. Eden had then persuaded Damiano to invite Cosetta to the twins' christening. Ignored by Damiano for months, his sister had been on her best behaviour and anxious not to cause offence. Eden was content to settle for politeness at their occasional meetings.

'*Dio mio.*' Damiano rhymed, turning from his now sleeping daughter to appraise Eden in her ball gown with deeply impressed eyes of gold. 'You look fantastic.'

Eden did a little twirl to ensure that he got the full effect of her bare shoulders and the low-cut back. He wolf-whistled. She grinned, her own attention roving with equally keen appreciation over his beautifully cut dinner jacket, silk shirt and narrow black trousers, all of which accentuated his commanding height, his athletic physique and his sheer sexiness. She tried really hard to wolf-whistle back but Damiano started laughing and she couldn't manage it.

'Happy, *cara mia*?'

'Absolutely fizzing with it!' Eden assured him cheerfully as he settled his hands to her slim waist and drew her into the circle of his arms. 'It's not every woman who gets to celebrate two wedding anniversaries a year!'

Exactly a year ago, they had renewed their wedding vows in a church ceremony which had meant a great deal to both of them. Damiano, however, also liked to celebrate their original wedding anniversary as well. Over fifty people were joining them for dinner that evening and a couple hundred more for a massive ball which would last until dawn.

Taking a last proud and loving look at their sleeping

children, they walked downstairs and strolled into the main salon, now furnished with far from authentic comfy sofas and armchairs. Damiano uncorked a bottle of champagne and sent it foaming into glasses.

'Shouldn't we wait for our first guests?' Eden enquired in surprise.

Damiano passed her a heart-shaped leather jewel case.

She flipped up the lid. Damiano could not apparently stand the suspense of waiting for her reaction and he reached out and lifted out the gorgeous sapphire and diamond pendant to turn it over to display the inscription.

'"To the only woman I have ever loved, Damiano",' Eden read out loud, her eyes misting over.

'I adore you, *tersoro mio*,' Damiano murmured huskily, fastening the beautiful necklace at the nape of her neck.

'I just *adore* the way you keep on telling me,' Eden whispered dreamily, spinning back to him, meeting his burnished eyes and just melting back into his arms. 'I love you too.'

VIVA LA VIDA DE AMOR!

They speak the language of passion.

In Harlequin Presents®, you'll find a special
kind of lover—full of Latin charm. Whether
he's relaxing in denims or dressed for dinner,
giving you diamonds or simply sweet dreams,
he's got spirit, style and sex appeal!

Latin Lovers is the new miniseries
from Harlequin Presents® for anyone
who enjoys hot romance!

Meet gorgeous Antonio Scarlatti in
THE BLACKMAILED BRIDEGROOM
by Miranda Lee, Harlequin Presents® #2151
available January 2001

And don't miss sexy Niccolo Dominici in
THE ITALIAN GROOM
by Jane Porter, Harlequin Presents® #2168
available March 2001!

Available wherever Harlequin books are sold.

HARLEQUIN®
Makes any time special ™

Visit us at www.eHarlequin.com

HPLATIN

He's a man of cool sophistication.
He's got pride, power and wealth.
He's a ruthless businessman, an expert lover—
and he's one hundred percent committed
to staying single.

Until now. Because suddenly he's responsible
for a BABY!

HIS BABY

An exciting miniseries from Harlequin Presents®
**He's sexy, he's successful...
and now he's facing up to fatherhood!**

On sale February 2001:
RAFAEL'S LOVE-CHILD
by Kate Walker, Harlequin Presents® #2160

On sale May 2001:
MORGAN'S SECRET SON
by Sara Wood, Harlequin Presents® #2180

And look out for more later in the year!

Available wherever Harlequin books are sold.

HARLEQUIN®
Makes any time special ™

Visit us at www.eHarlequin.com   HPBABY

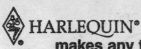

HARLEQUIN®
makes any time special—online...

eHARLEQUIN.com

your romantic books

♥ Shop online! Visit Shop eHarlequin and discover a wide selection of new releases and classic favorites at great discounted prices.

♥ Read our daily and weekly Internet exclusive serials, and participate in our interactive novel in the reading room.

♥ Ever dreamed of being a writer? Enter your chapter for a chance to become a featured author in our Writing Round Robin novel.

• • • • • • •

your romantic life

♥ Check out our feature articles on dating, flirting and other important romance topics and get your daily love dose with tips on how to keep the romance alive every day.

• • • • • •

your community

♥ Have a Heart-to-Heart with other members about the latest books and meet your favorite authors.

♥ Discuss your romantic dilemma in the Tales from the Heart message board.

your romantic escapes

♥ Learn what the stars have in store for you with our daily Passionscopes and weekly Erotiscopes.

♥ Get the latest scoop on your favorite royals in Royal Romance.

HINTA1

In March 2001,

presents the next book in

DIANA PALMER's

enthralling *Soldiers of Fortune* trilogy:

THE WINTER SOLDIER

Cy Parks had a reputation around Jacobsville for his taciturn and solitary ways. But spirited Lisa Monroe wasn't put off by the mesmerizing mercenary, and drove him to distraction with her sweetly tantalizing kisses. Though he'd never admit it, Cy was getting mighty possessive of the enchanting woman who needed the type of safeguarding only he could provide. But who would protect the beguiling beauty from *him…?*

Soldiers of Fortune…prisoners of love.

Silhouette®
Where love comes alive™

*Available only from
Silhouette Desire at
your favorite retail outlet.*

Visit Silhouette at
www.eHarlequin.com

SDWS

Getting down to business in the boardroom... and the bedroom!

A secret romance, a forbidden affair, a thrilling attraction...

What happens when two people work together and simply can't help falling in love—no matter how hard they try to resist?

Find out in our new series of stories set against working backgrounds.

Look out for

THE MISTRESS CONTRACT
by Helen Brooks, Harlequin Presents® #2153
Available January 2001

and don't miss

SEDUCED BY THE BOSS
by Sharon Kendrick, Harlequin Presents® #2173
Available April 2001

Available wherever Harlequin books are sold.

HARLEQUIN®
Makes any time special ™

Visit us at www.eHarlequin.com

HP925

Lindsay Armstrong...
Helen Bianchin...
Emma Darcy...
Miranda Lee...

Some of our bestselling writers are Australians!

Look our for their novels about the Wonder from Down Under—where spirited women win the hearts of Australia's most eligible men.

THE AUSTRALIANS

Coming soon:

THE MARRIAGE RISK
by Emma Darcy
On sale February 2001, Harlequin Presents® #2157

And look out for:

MARRIAGE AT A PRICE
by Miranda Lee
On sale June 2001, Harlequin Presents® #2181

Available wherever Harlequin books are sold.

HARLEQUIN®
Makes any time special ™

Visit us at www.eHarlequin.com   HPAUS